G R JORDAN

The Esoteric Tear

A Highlands and Islands Detective Thriller

First edition

ISBN: 978-1-915562-81-4

This book was professionally typeset on Reedsy.
Find out more at reedsy.com

Truth is a gem that is found at a great depth; whilst on the surface of the world all things are weighed by the false scale of custom.

Lord Byron

Contents

Foreword   iii

Acknowledgement   iv

Books by G R Jordan   v

Chapter 01   1

Chapter 02   10

Chapter 03   19

Chapter 04   28

Chapter 05   37

Chapter 06   47

Chapter 07   56

Chapter 08   65

Chapter 09   73

Chapter 10   82

Chapter 11   90

Chapter 12   100

Chapter 13   108

Chapter 14   116

Chapter 15   125

Chapter 16   132

Chapter 17   139

Chapter 18   147

Chapter 19   156

Chapter 20   164

Chapter 21   173

Chapter 22	180
Chapter 23	190
Chapter 24	199
Chapter 25	207
Read on to discover the Patrick Smythe series!	215
About the Author	218
Also by G R Jordan	220

Foreword

The events of this book, while based around real locations around Inverness, are entirely fictional and all characters do not represent any living or deceased person. All companies are fictitious representations. No eggs were cracked in the writing of this book!

Acknowledgement

To Ken, Jean, Colin, Evelyn, John and Rosemary for your work in bringing this novel to completion, your time and effort is deeply appreciated.

Books by G R Jordan

The Highlands and Islands Detective series (Crime)

1. Water's Edge
2. The Bothy
3. The Horror Weekend
4. The Small Ferry
5. Dead at Third Man
6. The Pirate Club
7. A Personal Agenda
8. A Just Punishment
9. The Numerous Deaths of Santa Claus
10. Our Gated Community
11. The Satchel
12. Culhwch Alpha
13. Fair Market Value
14. The Coach Bomber
15. The Culling at Singing Sands
16. Where Justice Fails
17. The Cortado Club
18. Cleared to Die
19. Man Overboard!
20. Antisocial Behaviour
21. Rogues' Gallery
22. The Death of Macleod - Inferno Book 1

23. A Common Man - Inferno Book 2
24. A Sweeping Darkness - Inferno Book 3
25. Dormie 5
26. The First Minister - Past Mistakes Book 1
27. The Guilty Parties - Past Mistakes Book 2
28. Vengeance is Mine - Past Mistakes Book 3
29. Winter Slay Bells
30. Macleod's Cruise
31. Scrambled Eggs
32. The Esoteric Tear
33. A Rock 'n' Roll Murder
34. The Slaughterhouse

Kirsten Stewart Thrillers (Thriller)

1. A Shot at Democracy
2. The Hunted Child
3. The Express Wishes of Mr MacIver
4. The Nationalist Express
5. The Hunt for 'Red Anna'
6. The Execution of Celebrity
7. The Man Everyone Wanted
8. Busman's Holiday
9. A Personal Favour
10. Infiltrator
11. Implosion
12. Traitor

Jac Moonshine Thrillers

1. Jac's Revenge
2. Jac for the People
3. Jac the Pariah

Siobhan Duffy Mysteries

1. A Giant Killing
2. Death of the Witch
3. The Bloodied Hands
4. A Hermit's Death

The Contessa Munroe Mysteries (Cozy Mystery)

1. Corpse Reviver
2. Frostbite
3. Cobra's Fang

The Patrick Smythe Series (Crime)

1. The Disappearance of Russell Hadleigh
2. The Graves of Calgary Bay
3. The Fairy Pools Gathering

Austerley & Kirkgordon Series (Fantasy)

1. Crescendo!
2. The Darkness at Dillingham
3. Dagon's Revenge
4. Ship of Doom

Supernatural and Elder Threat Assessment Agency (SETAA) Series (Fantasy)

1. Scarlett O'Meara: Beastmaster

Island Adventures Series (Cosy Fantasy Adventure)

1. Surface Tensions

Dark Wen Series (Horror Fantasy)

1. The Blasphemous Welcome
2. The Demon's Chalice

Chapter 01

J ohn Murray was having a bad day. When he'd taken the job, he had no idea it could ever turn out like this. After all, he was just going to stand there and watch people look at what they thought were precious diamonds. They weren't just diamonds, of course. They were gemstones of all different sorts. John didn't see any value, really, in them. But there were price tags attached.

These days, it wasn't the case that precious works of art remained in the capital cities. They went on tours, taken round to the public in all parts of Scotland, who could see them, revel in them, and get a bit of culture.

John couldn't give a stuff about that. What he cared about was it would give him a day's pay for standing around and doing nothing. A special van had been provided, more like an articulated lorry. Massive. And the public would walk through from one end out to the other, stopping on the way to see the precious gems concealed behind various see-through glass cages. If they were really lucky, somebody might come along and take a gemstone out and give them a really close look.

At least that was what the plan had been. That was until the trailer had started having power outages. Six times today, they had shut the trailer. Six times, John had to gone inside to ask people to step out of the trailer into the pouring rain. The articulated lorry was currently at Drumnadrochit, in the car park of the castle. The castle lay down below it and, in truth, there weren't that many people from the public daring to have a look.

Although the weather had driven many off, John wasn't sure if it was the weather that was causing the electrical connection to the lorry to have its problems. He wasn't that bothered that it was raining. If it kept the people away, all the better. However, what he was bothered about was so far he had eaten no lunch, having to remain close by—until they were sure the electric was finally back on.

John stood beside the lorry as the power was switched back on. He would give it ten minutes, give it a chance to see if it all was working. He turned, walked to the edge of the car park, and looked down at Urquhart Castle on the bank of Loch Ness. In its day, it would have looked splendid. Now, as a ruin, it was a tourist attraction, a neat car park above it and losing some of that quintessential rugged feel the castle originally would have had.

The castle was plonked on the side of the bank, a testament to man's ingenuity to build homesteads in some of the most awkward places. Nowadays, a perfectly good road ran down the side of Loch Ness. John wondered what Nessie would think of it if the legendary monster ever stepped out. *Had it seen changes down through the ages?*

'Oh, bugger,' said a colleague and John turned round instantly to see that the articulated lorry had failed again.

'That was less than a minute,' said John. 'What's going on?'

'I don't know. Maybe it's the rain. Loose connection? We're

working on it, John, okay?'

'Shut it up. Make sure it stays shut up, Okay? We can't be losing any of these gems.'

Walking towards John was a woman in her thirties. Ali Ralston had blonde hair that ran down the side of her neck. She was alluring, if a little too thin for John, but he'd worked with far more obnoxious people. Ali seemed a bit on edge, but maybe that was because she was responsible for taking all these gems on tour. When things didn't run smoothly, John could see that people would be bothered. He was, after all.

But people not going through the trailer meant less hassle for him. People not going through the trailer to Ali meant losing the purpose of being out here. And when the reports went back that the trailer was useless—that the trailer didn't provide a sensible space for people to view these gemstones— Ali would probably get it in the neck. John wasn't sure, but maybe she'd hired the trailer. Maybe she'd sorted the interior.

Inside, amongst the many cases of gemstones, were displays on the wall showing where different ones had come from. John hadn't been stuffed to read them. He wasn't like that. In fact, he wasn't into art at all. He was into getting his pay and going home. At the moment, it wasn't happening smoothly, and they could be here much longer.

'I think I've got it now,' said Mac. He was the senior electrician on site, although John wasn't sure how senior he'd ever got in his career. He certainly seemed to struggle with this problem.

'Okay, switch it on again.'

John heard a small zapping sound and the lights inside the trailer came on. They were visible through a small porthole in the door, and John looked inside. The gemstones, of course, hadn't moved. Still sitting there, now lit up, hopefully in all their glory. John unlocked the door and stepped inside. He spent the next ten minutes looking around, knowing that there was only one door in and one door out. The door at the far end opened.

'You're meant to knock. This is meant to be a secure area.'

'How's it meant to be secure if the door's open,' said Mac. 'I think it's holding now. I think I've got what was wrong with it.'

'Are you sure?' asked John.

'Well, I think so.'

Mac was slightly tubby, and John wasn't sure if the man had washed that morning. John, on the other hand, had a neat suit on, with a badge on the left-hand side saying 'Main Security Guard'. He had an ID pass and a belt which had many devices for incapacitating the public. Not that he'd ever been called to use them. This was a cushy number, but you had to look the part. You had to stand there and pretend that everything was life and death.

'You can open up then,' said Mac.

'Like bollocks am I'm going to do that,' said John. 'We've been on and off here all morning. What we'll do is we'll lock everything up, we'll leave the power running, we'll go get some lunch, and then we'll come back. If it's still running at that point, we'll declare it suitable to be opened and the public can spend all afternoon in here. Okay?'

'Well, you're the boss, but that connection's good,' said Mac.

'You've told me it's been good the last six times. Each time it's gone,' said John. 'And I'm starving. So, let's go get lunch. They can all wait. I'll be buggered if I'm going to miss my lunch so somebody can look at a piece of glass.'

'They're not strictly glass, are they?'

'Well, if they were just glass, they wouldn't be worth anything, would they?' said John.

He didn't know about diamonds, rubies, sapphires, emeralds, but he would not show his ignorance in front of Mac. So, he marched across the trailer, tapped Mac on the shoulder, indicating he should get out, and locked the door behind him. John walked round the trailer several times, locking the other end up, and disappearing off with the keys to find somewhere to have his lunch.

In a drizzling rain on the far side of the car park, John found a burger van with a rather disappointed looking woman inside. She was older than he, and she looked like she'd been working in burger vans all of her life. Not built trim like John, she probably had eaten a bit more than she should have done. But she had the look of someone who worked for a living. The eyes were tired, the shoulders slumped, and as John came forward, she failed to pick up at all.

'You got a burger and chips?' asked John.

'I'll cook you a fresh one. These last couple are just a disaster. Where on earth is everyone?'

'We've been having problems with the trailer. So, the ones that came at the start have all buggered off. Some have gone down to look at the castle. But the power's back on. We're running it until after I have my lunch. And if it's okay, then we'll open up.'

'It'll be after lunch then. Just brilliant. This is my best time. They were all meant to be here. Do you know how much this pitch has cost me?'

'No,' said John. 'What I do know is I ordered a burger. Burger and chips, can I get it?'

The woman looked at him with nasty eyes. John realised it might have been a bad idea to have said that. When people were making food, you didn't want to annoy them. You never know what they might do to the food. Was that the security mind working? Maybe. Always see the nasty side of things.

Mac came strolling over. 'Double burger and chips,' he shouted. 'And one of those Diet Cokes.'

'Diet Coke,' said John. 'What on earth do you want a Diet Coke for? I mean, get a grip. You've got enough calories in the burger. Why stop there.'

'It's always been Diet Coke. Helps me keep myself in shape,' said Mac. He slapped his belly with both hands, causing John to shake his head. John wasn't the most fit man alive, but he hadn't let himself go like Mac had. Women could still look at John and be pleasantly surprised. Who would want a slob like Mac?

That's why John got jobs like this. The man to be in charge. They didn't care about trouble. If you wanted actual security, you didn't hire the firm that John was from. You got proper security people to do it. People understood what people like John were about. John was here for show, here to make sure that the company could say, yes, there was security there, whatever happened. At a reasonable price. Reasonable meaning cheap.

His burger came along about five minutes later with some chips. John stood in the drizzle, throwing vinegar and salt onto his chips. He ate his lunch slowly, not desperate to rush, and found that Mac had eaten his by the time John had only got halfway through. Eventually though, he was finished, and had to return to the trailer.

John walked round the trailer and noticed Ali Ralston

looking at him. He smiled back. John wondered if she was going with the trailer to its next stop, or would she be in Inverness for the night? He walked over.

'Are we good to go?' asked Ali.

'Soon, I just need to do an inspection inside.'

'Okay,' said Ali. She stood expectant.

'You're not from round here, are you?' asked John.

'Kind of, but I've come up with the tour.'

'Right, what are you doing tonight? I hope you're going to pop out and see some of the Inverness nightlife.'

'The tour will move on, and I guess I'll move on with it.'

'Do you live near here?' asked John.

'Just north of Inverness.'

A local girl? thought John. *Interesting. If things went really well you never know what might happen.* 'Why don't I show you a few places in Inverness tonight?'

'Why don't you check the trailer so I can open it to the public before we lose the whole point of the day,' said Ali.

'All right,' said John, 'keep your hair on.' He turned away, grimacing. *So, she wasn't up for it. Pity,* he thought. *She looked a fine filly.*

He walked over to the trailer, up the steps at the side, and unlocked the door. John opened it and looked inside. The lights were still on and then his heart sank. The glass cases were there, but there was nothing inside them.

He ran inside, looking quickly from glass cover to glass cover. There were none. The emeralds, the sapphires, the rubies, the diamonds, they were all gone. But where? He ran over to the other side and tried the door, but it was locked. *How could that be? What on earth was going on?* He ran back to the other door, stepped outside.

'Have you done your check?' asked Ali.

'There's . . . there's . . .' John found he couldn't speak. He'd only gone for lunch. He'd gone maybe a hundred yards for lunch. By the time it had taken him to eat a burger and chips, they had all been swiped. They had all—

'Something wrong?' asked Ali.

'We need to call the police. 999. There's—they're all gone.'

'They're what?' blurted Ali. She stormed over, producing quite a stride despite the tight skirt she was wearing. 'What the hell do you mean, "they're all gone?"'

John watched her clatter up the stairs, inside the lorry, and then turn on her heel and come back out. 'They're all gone,' she said.

'I know they're all gone,' said John, reaching for his phone. He dialled 999, putting it up to his ear.

'Well, where are they?' shouted Ali. 'We can't have lost them all. We can't not have all these stones. Do you know how much these things are worth?'

'Of course I do,' said John, lying through his teeth. He had no idea. But they could pin it on him. They could blame him for it. Could he get sued? Could they do more than just sack him? John didn't know. He wasn't sure. He was panicking. Sweat started to pour down his face. He looked round and saw Mac coming towards him.

'See, the lights are still on,' said Mac. John just stared at him. Mac looked back, concerned. 'You all right?'

'All the stones, Mac. All of them. They've taken all of them.'

The phone in his hand talked almost from a distance at him.

'What service do you require?' said a voice. 'Sir? Madam? What service? Hello?'

John turned and looked at the trailer. His job was over. If he was lucky, he wouldn't be arrested. He would be arrested for uselessness, or whatever the correct word for it was. Meanwhile, Ali Ralston was looking at him.

'Just get the damn police,' she said. 'Hurry!'

But John just stood in complete disbelief. He'd only had a burger and chips.

Chapter 02

'I wish they would stop telling me I'm older,' said Clarissa, looking at the sign above the rack of clothing she was looking at. '"Trousers, for the older woman." What does that mean?'

Unless you were eighteen, you were always an older woman than someone. Besides, Clarissa wasn't old. Sure, the skin may look different. Sure, the body might have changed. Bits might have sagged. Parts of her might look as if they need ironed. But inside, she was as young as any of them. She could still kick as hard as the rest of them. She could still . . .

Clothes shopping was awful. Racks of sexy clothes that only the youngest and fittest could ever dream of. And then there was the expanded collection. For the oversized or the oddly shaped. It was never flattering.

Maybe she'd sit and have a coffee somewhere, go and relax. Frank would be finished from the club around about four. She thought they might go for a walk, maybe even go to the cinema. There were some wonderful films coming up.

It was something they'd begun to do. Pop out late in the afternoon or take an early evening flick. Frank had a rather extensive knowledge of cinema, something that had caught

Clarissa by surprise. She hadn't been married long to him, but they both had been sure of it, convinced it was the right thing to do. She wouldn't be alone for the rest of her life. Well, not unless he popped his clogs next week or something.

She laughed. It wasn't about that though, was it? She'd thought it had been. Clarissa had sought for someone. She hadn't been ready to give up all ideas of affection, all ideas of intimacy. She wanted someone to hold at night, and to hold her. Someone to go out and have fun with. But it had to be the right person.

Seoras had been there, and she'd thought about it, but the man, while not married, had a partner. And his partner wasn't going anywhere. And then Frank had come along. They golfed together. They did several things together, but they also spent time apart. It was good. It worked well for the both of them, and she was delighted about it.

Clarissa was in a better place than she'd been in for a long while. She was out of the murder squad, no longer arriving for the first day of work to see whatever carcass had been left behind. She was also now working with Patterson.

Eric, as he kept trying to tell her was his name, was far too good a detective to be stuck behind a desk. But the murder squad had affected him, and she couldn't blame Eric. He'd had his throat slashed and Clarissa had leaned on it and kept him alive, the blood all over her hands. Even now, as she checked the price of a pair of trousers, she could see them. It had nearly broken her.

His subsequent recovery had helped, but no longer would she visit dead bodies. She had been moved back to work on the Arts team. They weren't a big team. Several of them stationed in different parts of the country. Clarissa had a small office in Inverness as the detective inspector. She had a couple of sergeants elsewhere. They'd come together if needed, but most cases were small.

When the detail was filed up to Clarissa, she'd pass on juicy titbits to Macleod, who was acting as the DCI over all of them. He didn't have that much to do, to be honest. Which was a good job, because Seoras knew nothing about artwork. Absolutely nothing.

She could feel a vibration in her pocket and reached inside her tartan trews. She pulled out a small square object and looked down at the reading on it.

'Bollocks!' she exclaimed. So much so that half the shoppers in the store turned and looked at her. 'Buggery bollocks!' she said, aware that they were looking. 'It's work, flippin' work!'

Clarissa turned and strode off out of the store, heading back to her little green car. As she did so, she picked up her phone and called in to the desk sergeant.

'Got a load of stones stolen from Drumnadrochit.'

'You're having a laugh,' said Clarissa. 'That roadshow thing.'

'Yep. All of them. Gone. Not sure how they did it. I fired it in for Patterson, but he's not here at the moment. He's racing back to the station. We sent it out to you. Macleod said you were the right person for it, anyway.'

'Macleod would,' she said. 'If you see Patterson, tell him I'll be in ten to fifteen minutes and we head straight out.'

'Aye, all right,' said the desk sergeant.

Clarissa found her little green sports car parked in the multi-storey and jumped inside. She was three floors up, but she took them like she was on an indoor racetrack. She was still a skilful driver, even at this stage of her life, although she had a distinct awareness that none of her passengers believed her.

They saw her car as an eccentricity. What they didn't see was that this car could handle itself. She could take corners at a pace. Under the hood was a proper engine, and the handling was terrific. If those philistines couldn't see that, well, stuff them.

Clarissa knew one thing in life, quality. Quality in everything. She was more than aware of what the real value of things was. These gems out by Drumnadrochit, they weren't that big a deal. Heck, they were in a trailer, stuck on the side of a loch. If they were worth any real money, they'd have been brought up to the museum in Inverness. They'd have had an armed guard around them, and people would view them at a distance. Not that she agreed with that, either. Art needed to be seen up close—art needed to be handled.

Clarissa raced into the station car park and saw Patterson already standing at the rear doors. He had a suit on with a cravat which neatly covered up his neck wound. Clarissa liked it. She didn't want to see that neck wound every day.

That was mean of her, of course. He had to live with it every day of his life. But the cravat also gave him an arty look. Patterson had never said he was interested in art, but he could learn. He could get a passionate eye. Clarissa, of course, had been brought up as a bit of a trader as a young one, before becoming a police officer. She'd learned how to buy and sell, how to spot things that were worth real money at bric-a-brac sales.

But then she'd made a loss—a bad one—and been forced to take up a job as a police officer. She'd never been completely away from her love of culture and had manoeuvred herself back into the arts' side prior to her spell with Macleod. She'd enjoyed the murder team—she'd enjoyed the people around her—but she'd never felt comfortable with the dead bodies. And the time she saw those children. Clarissa felt herself shake, a shiver down her back, as Patterson stepped into the car.

'Hi, sunshine,' said Clarissa.

'My name's Eric. You know it's Eric.'

'I know, but sunshine always seems better. It's your bright and bubbly personality. You're like a piece of Italian dynamism.'

'I know you're my boss,' said Eric Patterson, 'but I really would rather we just get on with the case.'

'You got it, sunshine,' said Clarissa as she spun the little car. Two constables jumped out of the way as she tore out of the car park, shouting over her shoulder at them. 'Just got a job. Sorry!'

Patterson had always thought Drumnadrochit was a reasonable distance away. Either Clarissa had found a warp hole through which to drive, or the speed that she'd maintained on the way down, was truly impressive. Not being a man of particular sci-fi interest, Patterson was going with the latter.

'How did they lose them all?' asked Clarissa aloud as she drove. Patterson was hanging on to the door, bracing himself with his other hand. 'Don't do that,' said Clarissa. 'If we crash, you'll break your arm.'

'If we crash?' said Patterson. 'More like when.'

'There's no need to be cheeky. Besides, we'll take your car next time. We'll see how you drive.'

'No, you won't,' said Patterson. 'Last time I tried to drive, you did everything to make sure you drove. You're the DI, now. It's right that I should be driving. I should be the one driving you about so you have time to think.'

'I do my best driving when I'm thinking,' said Clarissa. 'Just you remember that, okay? And besides, I'm in charge. I'm driving.'

Patterson shook his head and Clarissa could see that his knuckles were white. He was gripping ever so tightly.

As the car sped along the road at the side of Loch Ness, they caught a first brief view of the castle. They were then taken briefly further inland around an inlet and then back out towards the castle, parking up in the car park. Clarissa could see there were only two police cars there at present.

'Let's get this show on the road,' she said to Patterson, opening her car door and storming across to a uniformed sergeant.

'Detective Inspector Urquhart.'

'Clarissa,' said DI Urquhart. 'Just Clarissa. What have we got?'

'Stolen about an hour to an hour and ten minutes ago. Well, at least that. Maybe earlier.'

'What do you mean earlier?'

'Security guard locked everything up, went for his lunch. When he came back, everything was gone from inside. He said the two doors were locked.'

'So, what are we looking at?'

'I don't know what we're looking at,' said the sergeant. 'It makes no sense whatsoever.'

'Okay,' said Clarissa, 'but assuming they're gone, where did they go? Have they gone north?'

'We got a roadblock out pretty quick, so we don't think so. We know a motorbike fled the scene. It was picked up by a tourist, disappearing in a hurry out to the south.'

'Why aren't we going that direction?' said Clarissa.

'Just trying to get enough people,' said the sergeant.

'Okay, fair enough.'

The radio on the sergeant's shoulder squawked to life. 'Another spotting of the bike at the turning at Invermoriston for Skye.'

'That's not that far down from here. And we've got units on the go,' said Clarissa.

She watched as the sergeant called it in. 'We got a couple of units near,' he said after speaking to some of them. 'They're heading out towards Skye, following it down that road.'

'You said it was a motorbike,' said Clarissa. 'What type?'

'What difference does the type make?' asked Patterson.

'Shush!' said Clarissa, waiting for the sergeant to reply.

'Scrambler type? A Yamaha, we think.'

'Scrambler type? Okay. We've got to get after it.'

'It's too much of a head start,' said Patterson. 'How are we going to catch up with it?'

'We'll take my car.'

'Oh, dear God,' said Patterson.

Clarissa was happy with the way the banter between the two of them was developing. Patterson was good for it, and he was teasing her a bit, delivering his own punches to her. Clarissa was always ready to call anyone out when doing their work, but Patterson did it too. He had done well, although they were still waiting for a big first case.

As she jumped in behind the wheel, Patterson joined her in the passenger seat, and hung on as she spun the wheel, raking out onto the road south.

'Invermoriston's just up here,' said Patterson, as they raced further down the road.

'I know where it is.'

'We want to be going right then.'

16

'How?' asked Clarissa.

'We want to be going right,' said Patterson.

'No, we don't,' said Clarissa. 'If we want to catch this guy, we are not going right.'

'Why? It's where everybody else is going.'

'Of course it is. That's the point, to send everybody off over there. Where's he going to go? That road leads out to Skye. He's going to hide everything in Skye? Or is he going to take a boat on the Minch? If he puts a boat on the Minch we'll stop him easy. It's slow. He'll be heading for Glasgow. He's going to head down the southern roads out towards Glasgow. I'll tell you that now.'

'But he's on a scrambler bike.'

'Of course he is,' said Clarissa. 'Why would you be on a scrambler bike if you didn't want to go off-road?'

'He hasn't gone off-road already.'

'That's because he's about to.'

'That's a hunch though, isn't it?' spat Patterson.

'It's experience,' said Clarissa. 'You've got to think like them, yeah? This guy's a thief. He's not a murderer, he's a thief. The man wants to get paid. He wants to hand this stuff off soon. You're going to go to Skye and do what with these jewels? He's either going to dump them with somebody there—let's face it, there's not that many who can handle these—or he's going to jump in a boat and head out into the Minch where he's bang to rights. He's heading for Glasgow, whether our uniformed friends think it or not.'

Patterson shook his head as the little green sports car raced by the junction.

'I guess we're committed now,' he said.

'You bet we are, and we're right. You trust me?'

'What?'

'I said, "Do you trust me?"' said Clarissa.

'No, we're never going to catch this motorbike.'

'Ten quid,' said Clarissa, putting out her palm and giving Patterson even more of a shock as she was now driving at speed with one hand. As a matter of fact, she wasn't even looking at the road—she was looking at him.

'Whatever,' he said, 'just watch the road.'

'The road's fine,' said Clarissa. 'It's doing okay. What's not doing okay is you. Keep your eyes peeled on the right-hand side. See if he's going to come back out. It's not an easy place to find people, but we also have to believe that if we can grab him now, we'll have these jewels back and be home in time for tea and biscuits.'

Clarissa threw her head back, laughing loudly. 'That'll be a first, won't it?' she said to Patterson. 'You're first on the crime team. I won't even make you describe what all the unique items are.'

'How valuable are they, though?'

Clarissa drove and thought. 'Not this valuable. It's not worth it. It just isn't worth it.'

The little green sports car raced on. Disappearing into the mid-morning. Clarissa was going to get him. If he'd taken the stuff, she was going to get him. After all, she'd spent enough time with her hair this morning. And the wind was ruining it. But these were her cases, and it was time to go bag her first thief.

18

Chapter 03

'Look, I'm telling you, there's no proper exit route out through Skye. They're walking into a world of trouble going that way. People who steal these things, they're clever. They either hide it close by, or they hasten. But they want to hurry with a lot of options. Turning out to Skye, there's like one or two roads, and they're not great roads. It's difficult to get away. If you jump in a boat, you're trapped between the islands and the mainland. There's no easy way out, Patterson; I'm telling you, they're not going on to Skye.'

'It was reported that they were going to Skye,' said Patterson. 'That's what the member of public said. That's where the police cars are going. They're in pursuit.'

'And do they have eyes on?' asked Clarissa.

'Not at this time. That's what they told me.'

'Then we're going on past the Skye turn off. We're going further down and we're going to see where it joins back onto the road.'

'Well, you're the boss.'

'Yes, I am,' said Clarissa, 'and I'll take the flack for it. Look, what have we got to lose? Everybody else is ahead of us. We will not catch up. As good as this car is, and I love it to bits, the rider's got much more of a head start. But why haven't they been seen? I mean, how long ago was that?'

'Maybe half an hour.'

'Exactly half an hour. They should have been well into Skye. They should be out of here before we even get near them. Instead, it's taking them a lot longer on a motorbike to get down there. Makes little sense. No sense at all. And why be seen? Why, when you take the gems, do you pop on a motorbike and run?'

'Because they're amateurs,' said Patterson. His hand went up to his hair, which, while cut short, was being buffeted in the wind. The top was down on the car—Clarissa, basking in the wind whipping past her face. Patterson seemed to think it was disturbing his neatly manicured hair.

She never would have said he was vain. He was just prim and proper. He liked things to be done correctly. Clarissa often wondered what he made of her. But here he was, out in the field. While he was debating with her, in truth he wasn't arguing. He wasn't saying she was wrong; he was just pointing out all the other alternatives. However, if she was wrong about this, and should not get an arrest, Macleod would probably give her a word or two.

The little green car whizzed down the road, overtaking several other cars. Clarissa saw Patterson's hand go out several times towards the dash in front of him. He hung on to the door when she swung back into the correct lane after overtaking on a particularly hairy bend. She knew the car; she knew what was safe and what wasn't, and she wasn't wholly reckless. In fact, she wasn't reckless at all. Just a damn excellent driver. And she was sick of the comments that she wasn't. After all, she could outrun any of them in this little baby.

Clarissa looked around the little green car at the little touches that had made it hers. She was grateful Macleod had restored it. He'd repaired it after she'd nearly lost it in the line of duty. When the day came to retire, this little one was coming with her.

The pair had passed the junction that broke off towards Skye at Invermoriston, Clarissa continuing farther south. Now a road joined back in from Skye, and she drove about five hundred yards past and then parked up

'What are we waiting here for?'

'We're waiting here, Patterson, because someone's going to come out there.'

'He's going to come out when?' asked Patterson.

'When he's well assured that the police are well into Skye. He'll want to circle back when they are committed.'

'I think you're reading this wrong,' said Patterson.

'Really, Pats? How's that?'

Clarissa liked the word Pats. She had a thing where she liked to call people by her own version of their name. She didn't do that with Seoras. He wouldn't have gone for it. Hope was too buttoned up. But Als, Als was too polite to complain. Everyone else called him Ross. But Al's gave him that little touch of panache. And so, with Pats. He was Pats now, anyway, because he had the cravat. He didn't look as buttoned up tight as he had before.

'He'll come out here, Pats. You wait and see. You need to think about the robbery. Okay?'

'In what way? Somebody's just grabbed a load of jewels and legged it. Legged it on a motorbike.'

'There's been power outages all day. Problems with the wagon,' said Clarissa. 'Then this guy disappears off for his lunch. He comes back, everywhere's locked up. That's not an impromptu grab. They've gone and taken the stuff and then come out the other side, locking everything back up again. They've done it when everyone's gone to lunch.'

'But they've grabbed everything. I mean, they don't know what they're looking at, do they?'

'Why?' asked Clarissa. 'If you're a thief, what are you going to do? You're going to take everything. You don't want people to know what you're after. That collection in there, I looked at it the other week when it was coming this way. There are a couple of suitable pieces but they'd be taken by a moderate sort of thief. People who would know what to do with it. They wouldn't jump on the back of a bike and leg it. And if they're jumping on the back of a bike and legging it, they'd have left the door open. They wouldn't have locked up again. There's too much that's not sitting correctly here,' said Clarissa.

'I'll have to take your word for that,' said Patterson. 'I don't have the experience of—'

'No, you don't,' said Clarissa. 'So, trust me on this one. But use that brain of yours. You're not daft; you're good, okay, so trust me on this.'

They sat looking down the road, Clarissa occasionally looking in the rear-view mirror, as an occasional car would draw past,

'What makes you think he will not get into a car?' asked Patterson

'Because I think he's on his own. May be a she, of course. Easier that way. You've got somebody else coming to meet, too easy to screw it up.'

'But what about the bike?' said Patterson. 'People are going to recognise the bike.'

'They're going to look for the bike on Skye. He's going to be down the road heading south. Oh, he'll get rid of the bike eventually, but he'll get some distance in first. He won't leave his car sitting around near the robbery site. If a car is left sitting around, it gets noticed, especially in places like this. It's not busy enough to leave a car, unless you hide it very well.

'No, he's going to use the bike to cross from the first Skye road back out. At some point, he's going to break off, and he's going to get through the countryside back to the more southerly road coming out of Skye. That way, they've never lost him. He's still on the road to them.'

'Why don't they think of this?'

'Because they're in pursuit. He's fleeing. He's doing something strategic,' said Clarissa.

They sat there for another twenty minutes. The police cars would be well into Skye now. Possibly racing through Portree, out further, maybe. Maybe towards Dunvegan, maybe out towards Uig.

'You still think you're right?' asked Patterson.

'I'm right,' said Clarissa. 'Here, you want a sweet?' She reached over and opened the glove box compartment, pulling out some boiled sweets. She handed the bag to Patterson. 'Go on, imagine you're back to being a kid.'

Clarissa took one out herself, popped it into her mouth, and sucked on it noisily while Patterson had one. She looked as if she was just glancing left and right, enjoying the view. And then someone shot past her, on a green motorcycle. It was of the scrambler variety.

Before Patterson could react, Clarissa had turned the engine on, spat her sweet out onto the roadside and the car was off. Patterson nearly choked on his sweet, but Clarissa didn't care.

She was on the way, hurtling as quick as she could.

'I told you,' she said, shouting over the noise of the car racing along. The road south from the Skye junction bent left and right. Not your average A-class road, but a tight one, with bends here and there, through woods, up and down, by the side of the lochs.

The man on the bike was clearly aware he was now being pursued. Clarissa hoped he was panicking, hoped he didn't know what to do. As she hammered along in the car, she watched in front of her, and saw the man take off a backpack he was wearing. As he rode across a small bridge, he turned and flung the backpack off into the water.

Clarissa slammed her brakes, pulled over quickly, and shouted at Patterson, 'Out! Go get it! Go get that bag!'

Patterson jumped out, and before he closed the door, the car was on its way again, the passenger door swinging shut violently as she tore off. In the rearview mirror, she saw Patterson racing down in towards the water, but Clarissa had no time to watch him. The rider had a short steal on her now, but her car had more to give than people reckoned.

She drove quickly, getting up behind him, following him as he overtook one car, then another round dangerous bends. Getting up close behind him, she touched wheels; she saw his bike spin left and right slightly. He slammed on the brakes and went down an embankment at the side of the road. Clarissa pulled the car up, watching the man leap off, falling on the ground.

Clarissa was wearing her shawl and tartan trews but had solid boots on underneath. She didn't quite jump sprightly down the bankside, but sort of stumbled down until she reached the bike where the man was getting to his feet. He had a motorcycle helmet on, and she got in between him and the bike. In truth, she hadn't really planned for this. Patterson should be with her. Patterson could help her take the man down. Looking at him now, he was at least her height, looked physically strong, and the helmet wasn't coming off. She might try to feint a move, wind him. She wasn't sure quite what to do.

The man didn't give her an opportunity to think any further. He ran at her. Clarissa stepped to one side, catching him with a low punch into his stomach. The man was clearly strong, and it didn't affect him much. The palm of his hand caught her hair. He pulled her down, and went to drive a knee into her face.

She struggled, though, and the knee ended up connecting with her shoulder, enough to spin her and send her tumbling to the ground. She tried to recover quickly, tried to roll back to her feet, but ended up on her back, her hands going up, waiting for the follow-up. But instead, she heard the roar of the bike.

'No, you don't,' she shouted, trying to haul herself up to her feet, but the bike was already on its way up the bankside, heading off down the road. Clarissa went to race after it, but the blow she'd taken was more than she'd expected, and she fell back down to her knees. She was panting.

Hell, she thought, '*hell, he's gone, need to...* She reached for her phone, hauling it out from the depths of her shawl. She rang the station and got the desk sergeant.

'South of Invermoriston, tell them they're going the wrong way,' said Clarissa. 'He's still on the green bike. He's still going south. Get units to come up from the south. He'll not be on it for long. He knows he's rumbled.'

'Yes, Inspector,' said the voice on the other end.

Clarissa then closed the call and slowly made her way up the side of the bank until she got into the car. The bike was gone. She would not follow it now. He would have several minutes, if not five, ahead of her. She wouldn't catch him.

He'd cut off somewhere and head into the distance. If he stayed on the road, he was an idiot, and they'd catch him. But this man wasn't an idiot.

She spun the car around and slowly made her way back up to the bridge where the bag had been flung. Sitting at the roadside on his bottom was Patterson, a bag beside him. She looked at the map. It was the William Arrol bridge. *Well, you learn something every day,* she thought. *I never knew it had a name.*

'You get it, Pats?'

'Yes,' he said, and walked over to the car, handing the bag to her. Patterson circled around the rear of the car before climbing in on the passenger seat. 'You lose him?'

'I failed to apprehend him,' said Clarissa. 'We had a fight. Could have done with you.'

'You told me to get the bag.'

'I did,' said Clarissa. 'And you did it well. Let's get back up as we need to do an inventory on these.' Clarissa opened the bag and looked. 'Yeah, they're probably all there.'

'I don't think the bag was open when I got it,' said Patterson. 'Couldn't see any lying around on the grass. I did a bit of a search.'

'You're not daft, are you, Pats? Anyway, let's get back up to our crime scene. Somebody there will tell us if they're all in here. But even if we don't get him, at least we will have recovered these. I mean, their value is pretty low.'

'Low?' said Patterson. 'What do you mean by low?'

'Well, that one there,' said Clarissa, holding a ruby up into the light. 'Five grand?'

'Five grand! And that's low?'

'Yeah,' said Clarissa. 'Trust me. That's low.'

Chapter 04

The green car pulled up back at Urquhart castle. Clarissa noted Pats was shaking his legs.

'What's up?' she asked.

'Well, the thing is that I had to go into the water to get the bag. Shoes got covered.'

'And you haven't complained once. That's quite something. Do you know that? See the murder team, they'd have complained all right. They'd have wanted to get a change. They'd have—'

'You don't need to keep talking about them,' said Patterson. 'Don't keep referring to it.'

'Why?' asked Clarissa, suddenly going serious.

'Whenever we talk about it, when you mention the team. It brings it back. It brings back the whole, well, the knife incident.'

'So what do I do? Just not . . .'

'Don't call them the murder team. Don't call them the—just don't call them. Call them by name. I don't mind you saying Ross or Hope, Susan Cunningham, you know—the names are fine. That doesn't make me think of that. I think of the person. As soon as you say the murder team, I think of the case. I think of what happened.'

'Okay,' said Clarissa.

She thought he was doing better than that. But then again, what did she know? She wasn't a psychiatrist, after all. She didn't know him. Whether he was better or not, he had come a long way. She had seen the scar around his neck, the one that wouldn't go away, the one that was now being hidden with a cravat. He seemed to enjoy the flamboyant piece of clothing.

'Do you want to get changed?' asked Clarissa.

'And how do I do that?'

'Well, I've got wellies in the boot. You know, you can wear my wellies.'

'And what shoe size are you?' asked Patterson. Clarissa looked down at her feet and looked over at Patterson's.

'We need to have a carry bag.'

'No,' said Patterson.

'What do you mean, no? I'm the boss. I said we need a carry bag.'

'You had a carry bag in your boot on the murder team because you'd get called. You'd possibly be away for a day, a night, two nights before you got back. Blouses lying around because you might need them, because you never got away from the place. No, we need to operate differently.'

'Well then, you just need to put a pair of wellies in my boot, all right? Look, Pats. I know you want us to be different, and we'll be different. And we'll make it different. But at the end of the day, we still need to have stuff with us. We can still get called out, might have to jump off and go to a museum somewhere. We might have to run down south. Just because we're operating out of Inverness doesn't mean we will not join the rest of the Arts team at a moment's notice. We need a—'

'Overnight bag,' said Patterson. 'It's an overnight bag. Not a carry bag. It's not a grab bag. It's an overnight bag.'

'Okay. It's an overnight bag,' said Clarissa. 'What's the difference?'

'An overnight bag is planned. It's just a change of clothing. It's got nothing to do with the murder team.'

Clarissa stared at Patterson's eyes. He was deadly serious. She nodded. If this was what it was going to take to bring him back, to get him functioning fully, then so be it. She felt a responsibility for him.

Frank had asked her why. After all, she'd saved his life. She hadn't sliced the knife along his throat. She was the one who'd helped him get back to where he was now. Clarissa didn't see it like that. She'd been the sergeant at the time. Patterson had been her responsibility.

'Let's go then,' said Clarissa. 'But don't squeak on me in those shoes.' Patterson laughed. 'They won't be looking at you anyway,' said Clarissa. 'They always look at me when I walk in. More stylish. You've just got a boring suit.'

She didn't look at him as she stepped out of the car, but she hoped he was grinning at that. That was a lot of it, wasn't it? Take the focus away from him. Take the focus away from what he was doing. Put the focus on work. Put the focus on her. After all, she was a new DI. She was being watched.

Clarissa strode over to where the uniformed sergeant was negotiating with several of his officers.

'Clarissa,' he said, seeing her again. 'We've got some people coming up from the south, I hear.'

'They'll not get him. Gave me a crack on the shoulder but we got these,' she said, and turned to point back at Patterson. He held the bag up in front of him.

'Well done. At least you've got the goods back. Miss Ralston will be quite happy about that.'

'What's her full name?'

'Ali Ralston.'

'Well, I need to speak to her now and I'll need to go through what's in this bag. Can you find her for me?'

'Derek,' the man shouted over to one of his officers, 'go get Miss Ralston, please. Ask her to go into the back of the forensic van. I'm sure you'll be all right in there.'

Clarissa nodded at Patterson and together they walked over to the forensic van, where Jona was stepping out of the back of it.

'You don't get away from me, do you?' said Jona. 'And you've . . . why isn't that in a nice bag?'

'That's been in the loch. We've just fished it out,' said Clarissa.

'What's in it?'

'What was nicked, Jona. I need to take them out and get our expert to have a look at them. Miss Ralston's going to be joining us in the back of your van.'

'Oh absolutely,' said Jona. 'Not even a by-your-leave? Not even a "Can we use your space, Jona?"'

'Excuse me? You're talking to the DI here,' said Clarissa, grinning at Jona, who laughed.

'Of course, you can use the back of it. Give me the bag and I'll put it on the table. I'll get geared up and I will lift the stuff out. Okay? Meantime, I want you suited up.'

'You're bossing me,' said Clarissa.

'I don't care if you're a DI. I don't care if you're the Pope. You're getting suited up. If you're going in to look at this stuff.'

Clarissa led Patterson round to the back of the forensic truck. They pulled out some coverall suits. Knowing she was going to be inside for a while, Clarissa took off her tartan shawl, and clambered inside the coverall suit, before putting a net over her hair. Patterson soon joined her as Miss Ralston approached, led forward by Derek.

'Thank you, officer,' said Clarissa. 'I presume you're Miss Ralston, Ali Ralston?'

The blonde-haired woman looked back. 'Yes, I am, and you are?'

'Detective Inspector Clarissa Urquhart. This is DC Eric Patterson. We've just recovered your jewels. They're inside this van, and we're going to take a look at them. I request you put on one of these coverall suits. I need you to identify the items and make sure they're all here.'

'How did you get them?' the woman asked.

'We tracked down the man who disappeared off on the bike. Long story short, I shoved him down a bank, but not before he flung these jewels into the loch side in the bag. My intrepid constable leapt in to save the jewels. I went to stop the man and took a good kicking because of it. He's disappeared, but I think we've recovered all the jewels.'

'Well, absolutely, I'll take a look,' said Ali. 'That's fantastic.'

Clarissa watched, not convinced that the woman thought it was that fantastic. Jona approached, having gone off to supervise some of her people.

'Right,' she said. 'If we're all ready, I'll go inside.'

'Miss Ralston's just putting her coverall suit on. Pats, you stay with her and bring her in when she's ready. I'll go on ahead with Jona.'

Jona turned to Ali Ralston. 'I'm Jona Nakamura, the Chief Forensic Officer. Just follow what DC Patterson says and we'll see you inside. Don't worry, I know how to handle items like these. And I'd ask that you don't touch them. Or if you want to, ask me first and I'll make sure that you can touch them in a way that doesn't interfere with our forensic processes.'

Jona entered the wagon, followed by Clarissa, who was told to stand in one corner while Jona prepared a table and took the bag. She photographed it first from all sides, carefully opened it, and took out the jewels from within.

'Do you know how many there are meant to be?' said Jona.

'Not exactly,' said Clarissa. 'Around twenty, I think.'

'You are the DI on this, aren't you? You don't even know how much stuff's been nicked.'

'I have just legged it down the road, taken a knee to the shoulder, and recovered the jewels. That's why I'm the DI. I'm not here for the numbers.'

Jona laughed. And then went quiet as Patterson opened the door of the wagon and entered with Ali Ralston.

She's quite attractive, Clarissa thought. *Tall and thinnish, but with a shape that men would like.* She wanted to know if she was any good at her job, though. Clarissa had been to many places, seen many types of people working in the arts industry. Some had blagged their way there and didn't really know what they were talking about. Others were absolute experts. Some had used their physical looks to get to where they wanted to be. Others had used their smarts, while some had used money, influence, and family. Clarissa was always wary when someone was introduced as the expert or the facilitator. *Did they really know what they were doing, or were they just a promotions person?*

'If you put the items out on the table, we'll get Miss Ralston to identify them,' said Clarissa.

'If you'll all stand back, I'll photograph them first.'

Gloved up, Jona carefully removed each of the jewels, placing them on the table in front of her. She then took her camera and photographed them and began measuring them, careful not to touch them.

'Can I get Miss Ralston to have a look?' said Clarissa impatiently.

'Absolutely,' said Jona, 'but don't come too close and don't pick them up,' said Jona.

'There should be twenty-one jewels here,' said Ali.

'Then we're one short,' said Patterson. Clarissa was taken aback. She counted them. He was right. There was only twenty there.

'Do you know which one's missing?' Clarissa asked Ali.

She watched the woman stare over the jewels. Her finger was floating, pointing toward one jewel, then the next. She was clearly counting in her head as her finger bounced from one jewel to the other.

'Oh, thank God,' said Ali, suddenly.

'What?'

'The Russian Fire, it's there. That emerald on the far side, the Paradise Emerald, it's there. They're the two most expensive items.'

'How much?'

'Twenty thousand, probably, estimated.'

'So, what's missing?' asked Clarissa.

'It's a large diamond. It's big, but it's not expensive. A couple of thousand, I think, at the last valuation we saw of it.'

'And it's in the collection because . . .?' asked Patterson.

'Because this is a collection that has a lot of backstory that's tied into myths and legends. The one that's missing is the Esoteric Tear, and its history is quite shaded. It's to do with the end of the world. Originally, I believe it came from a

Sanskrit book, but the accurate history of it is quite faded. It's an apocalyptic diamond, although we're not sure what it was to do with.'

'Why is it here?'

'Because it is tied into a long-forgotten civilisation. That much we know, the real history beyond that we don't. To be honest, it kind of got added because, well, it needed to. It hadn't surfaced until recently and the Scottish museums were quick on to it. Surprisingly quick.'

'What, there was some end of budget funding or something,' said Clarissa. Patterson glanced over at her. 'It's not uncommon,' said Clarissa. 'I'm not being negative.'

'Maybe it just fell out,' said Ali.

'Fell out?' asked Jona.

'Maybe it fell out of the bag down by the loch. Do you have divers or people who can have a look?'

'I can certainly get down. Where was it?' asked Jona.

'If you keep going down until the William Arnold Bridge, it was down there. Patterson could give you a better idea of where he walked. Worth you going down, Pats, with Jona, showing her where you were.'

'I didn't think the bag had opened though, but looking at it,' said Jona, 'that top's not fully secure. How big's the diamond?'

Ali Ralston held up her fist. 'Slightly smaller than that,'

'Well, we'll have a look at it,' said Jona. 'I'll look after these. Obviously they'll get returned to the museum, but I want to check for fingerprints, etc,'

'Well, thank you, Miss Ralston; that'll be all at the moment,' said Clarissa.

'No, no, thank you, and I'm just grateful it's only the Esoteric Tear that's missing. It's probably the lowest valued item we have here. I could probably get it on the insurance. It won't make that much of a difference. Thank you for getting this back. I think I would have been in real trouble if they'd all gone missing.'

'Pats, please escort Miss Ralston outside,' said Clarissa 'I want a quick word with Jona here.'

Clarissa watched Patterson take Ralston outside and then turned to Jona.

'What?' asked Jona. 'You don't look happy.'

'Have a look. Check for this diamond. I think we're getting played.'

'In what way?'

'It's a hunch, a feeling. The cheapest one happens to be gone. The one nobody will care about. He flung the bag. I wasn't on him at that point. He may still have got away. I don't get it.'

'You're the detective. You do the thinking on that one. Me, I'm taking Patterson down. We're going to seal off that site and if it's there, we'll find it. And then you can stop doing all your thinking. Instead, go after whoever nicked this.'

Jona left the forensic wagon, but Clarissa stood and looked at the diamonds. These were more valuable, but he gave them up. The arts world was such that sometimes value wasn't everything. Sometimes the value of something wasn't necessarily in currency.

Clarissa began to sweat. *Forensic wagons are always stuffy*, she thought. She stepped outside, unzipped out of the coverall, and put her shawl back on. She'd get her shoulder looked at because it was still sore and then she'd sit down and have a think. Something was bugging her, something was up.

Chapter 05

C larissa walked around her office, staring one minute out of the window—but never looking at any of the fixtures outside—then back inside the next. She turned again, now staring at the wall, on which was a timescale of some improvements she felt she could make to the Arts team.

There were various coordinated days when they would come together from their different areas. Clarissa was already planning an away day. She wasn't so old school that she didn't see the benefit of some of these practices, but she knew she wouldn't be getting the largest budget. Art thefts were all right—they happened to wealthy people. Often insurance brokers were involved or insurance investigators for the larger items, working allegedly alongside the police. At times, they would drain your resources and not give a lot of their own. After all, if the police found everything, what would be the point in asking a private investigator to come in?

Clarissa stepped outside the office and made coffee at the little kitchenette in the corridor. It wasn't like the murder team where they were so big they had their own unit. In fact, she shared the kitchen area with a couple of other teams. She looked down at some of the sugar spilt beside the sink. Turning on her heel, she marched round and banged on the door of an adjacent office.

'I swear, Lauritson,' she shouted, 'you leave sugar like that next time, I'm going to throw the damn sugar at you.'

The door opened, and a startled man looked at her. 'That's not my sugar. I take brown. I don't know who left it there. So don't—'

Clarissa wasn't listening. She had turned her back, and was pouring her own coffee before making her way back into the office.

How this robbery was conducted didn't seem right. It was wrong. There were teams now searching the lochside at the William Arrol Bridge, but Clarissa wasn't hopeful of finding anything. *It never fell out of the bag.*

Of course, they had to look at it. Of course, they had to check. But it was wrong. There was nothing coming out of that bag. Somebody stole the Esoteric Tear for a reason. It was the cheapest item. It wasn't worth much and yet somebody wanted it.

She hadn't been happy about Ali Ralston's explanation of the history of the Tear. And anyway, had she said it correctly? Was it sounding like T-ear, as in what comes from your eyes, or like T-air, as in to rip something apart? Diamonds were sometimes shaped like tears, though this one didn't seem to be so. Clarissa had obtained a photograph, but the trouble with photographs was they didn't do justice to jewels. You needed to see them in the flesh. You needed to appreciate them.

Quite what this one was, she didn't know, but somebody had wanted it. Somebody had wanted it enough to stage, as she thought, a rather bizarre robbery. To make it look like it was lost. Why?

She needed to know more of the history. Clarissa put her mug down on her desk and marched out of her office and up the stairs. As she reached the top, she saw Macleod's secretary.

'Is he available?'

'He's doing some paperwork. I can schedule a meeting.'

'He's available then. Good.' Clarissa marched forward, pushed open the door and rapped on it after it had already swung open.

'I'm just doing some paperwork,' said Seoras Macleod, sitting behind his desk. His eyes were focused angrily on her. 'Do you know how long I take to get through this stuff? I need peace and quiet.'

'I need to go to London.'

'What do you mean you need to go to London?' asked Macleod.

'I need to go to London. I want to take Patterson with me. He could do with coming. He'll learn a lot.'

'You've got a case on. It's up here.'

'This is to do with the case. I need to understand the history of this diamond.'

'Which diamond? There were twenty plus diamonds or rubies or whatever they are.'

'No, there's twenty recovered, thanks to me,' said Clarissa. 'There's one missing.'

'I thought they were fishing in the loch for it.'

'It won't be there.'

'How do you know that?' asked Macleod. He'd pushed the paperwork to one side now and was standing up behind his desk.

'Because,' said Clarissa, 'it's the one they were after.'

39

'How do you know that?'

'It's cheaper than all the rest and it's the one that's gone missing. You wouldn't have taken this lot as a collection. You'd have to be pretty amateur to have got rid of them in that way. They locked up the trailer afterwards. The whole thing makes little sense. It's not smooth. It's not a proper robbery.'

'They ran off, disappeared off on a bike, and then attacked you when you tried to stop them. They ditched the stuff. It looks like a smash and grab. A quick—'

'No, it's not,' spat Clarissa. 'There were power cuts before. Things were up, but somebody waited until lunchtime, waited until they could get in and get out.'

'Did you check the access to the trailer?' asked Macleod.

'Several people had access, but people you would have trusted because they were bringing the items on tour.'

'People like who?' asked Macleod.

'People like Ali Ralston. Like our security guard, like just about everybody. I mean, there was, yes, a significant amount of money on show, but not ridiculous. The items that go on these roadshows, they're not the Mona Lisa.'

'I can't send you to London.'

'But I want to go to London.'

'Look,' said Macleod. 'Jane currently wants to go to the Bahamas. But like you, she will not be funded by this police force. She will be funded by my wages. You will be funded—'

'Oh, come on, Seoras. This is something to get our teeth into. This is real. Big!'

'Where's the evidence? Where is it?'

'It's instinct. Tell me you don't go on instinct.'

'I don't sign my claim forms and my requests for travel by instinct,' said Macleod.

Someone appeared at the door of the office and Clarissa saw Macleod wave him in. It was a private conversation, but on turning, she saw it was Patterson.

'Eric,' said Macleod, 'your boss here says you need to go to London.'

'If the boss says so, must be right.'

'You're talking to me,' said Macleod, 'don't give me pat answers, okay? Why is she wanting to go to London?'

'First that I've heard of it,' said Patterson.

'You haven't even talked it over with him. You seriously telling me you haven't talked it over with Eric, yet you want to take him?'

'Can I just say something?' asked Eric.

'If you do,' said Clarissa, 'it better be bloody good.'

'Look, Detective Chief Inspector.'

'Don't! Don't use the title. The title will get you nowhere.'

Patterson gave an apologetic nod. 'We wouldn't have caught up with this thief if it wasn't for Clarissa. Everybody else was racing off after the bike to Skye. She was waiting for him. She knows the arts world, knows the arts people. I don't. If she wants to go to London, it's for a reason.'

'We're going to find out the accurate history of this item. The Esoteric Tear is at the core of this,' said Clarissa.

'Sounds reasonable to me,' said Eric.

'Fine. Go. Book your hotel. Book your expenses. Whatever,' said Macleod. Clarissa turned and smiled at Eric, pumping a fist. But as they left the room, Macleod shouted after them. 'And by the way, if this is a dud, Eric, you're paying.'

Eric looked at Clarissa. She waved her hand. 'I know what I'm doing,' she said, marching out of the office.

To save time, Clarissa caught a flight with Eric that evening

41

down to London, stopping in a hotel in the centre of town. At nine a.m. the next morning, they were on the south bank of the Thames, looking at the working river in front of them. Boats were travelling up and down the murky water.

'It's not the prettiest, is it?' said Eric, looking at the water.

'Have you ever been in Paris and seen the Seine? This here is paradise, trust me.'

Eric looked around him. 'Who's your friend?'

'My friend is Edmund Farrier and Edmund knows everything about everything. He hears the rumours. He's got connections.'

'Is he legit?'

'When you say is he legit?' asks Clarissa. 'What do you mean by that?'

'I mean, is he a proper dealer or does he—'

'We're going to have to change the terminology, all right? If you don't get caught for it, it's not illegal in a lot of the art world. Things are stashed away. People have private collections. Okay? So don't get into that. Edmund is a decent guy. Okay? He does nothing too illegal. Doesn't hurt people. He doesn't coerce people. He might cheat the odd one if he thinks he can get away with it. But he knows the limits well. Don't worry, he's a good guy.'

They stood for another ten minutes before Clarissa pointed at a man walking towards them. He was tall, with a cane and a slap of grey hair whispering across his temple beneath a brown hat. He wore a waistcoat with a suit jacket on the outside.

'Clarissa, darling, it was good to hear you were back in this game. Not looking at all those bodies.'

'Edmund, it's a pleasure.' Clarissa held her hand forward and Edmund took it and kissed it. She then turned, pointing at Eric.

'This is Eric Patterson.'

'This is Detective Constable Eric Patterson,' said Edmund. 'Alive today because of our heroic Clarissa. Funny how you've teamed up together. I hope you're not trying to murder the poor man.'

'I am actually here,' said Eric. 'Pleasure to meet you, sir.' His hands shot forward and took Farrier's. Patterson had a surprisingly powerful grip, and it caused Farrier to wince slightly.

'Very good. Shall we repair to somewhere? Spot of tea, maybe?'

'When did you ever have a spot of tea in the morning?' asked Clarissa.

'Well, there are no pubs open at this time.'

'Indeed, not,' said Clarissa.

Ten minutes later, they were sitting on a balcony of a small hotel overlooking the river. In front of Clarissa sat a glass of champagne, one beside her for Eric, and a large gin and tonic was being consumed by Edmund.

Clarissa leaned over to Eric, whispering in his ear, 'If you tell me we're on duty and shouldn't be having this, I will personally throw you into that river.' She stopped and turned back to Edmund Farrier. 'Edmund, you need to help me,' she said.

'If I can, without sacrificing myself in the process. What can I help you with, dear lady?'

'The Esoteric Tear.' Farrier's face fell.

'Tell me you're not mixed up in that.'

'I'm on the trail,' said Clarissa, 'and I want to know its history.'

'Certain groups are looking for it at the moment,' said Edmund, 'and I won't mention them. I know it by rumour, but

I haven't looked into it. You can't buy the Esoteric Tear.'

'Why?'

'Somebody within the Scottish Museum system has blocked it, quite cleverly. It's not up for sale. National treasure, something to be looked after.'

'But it's nothing. It's a knick-knack.' said Clarissa. 'It's only worth a couple of grand.'

'The Tear brings disaster around it. Do you know what it's for?'

'Looking at,' said Eric.

'Oh, dear boy,' said Edmund. 'If you're going to be in this art world, and I understand you haven't before, you need to understand that the story is so much more than the object.'

'But there is no history with it. No actual history. That's why it's so cheap,' said Eric.

'There is a history with it, if you know where to go, who to ask. That diamond is well sought after. People would pay savagely for it. But, at the moment, it cannot be purchased. Therefore, they will go after it. I heard it was on tour.'

'Not anymore,' said Clarissa. 'It's gone. Stolen amongst a lot of other gems and then, mysteriously, when the backpack containing these gems was thrown into the loch, the Tear disappeared.'

'Hmm,' said Farrier. 'That's not good.'

'And does sound like it T-ear, as in water from your eyes, or T-air, as in to rip apart?' asked Clarissa.

'T-air, the rip. Doesn't look like a tear,' said Farrier. 'But that's not where the name comes from. If I were you, I'd look at Ali Ralston. She organised the trip up there. There were no plans for the diamond to go anywhere. But it was cheap and added in. It made sense for the tour, I guess. However, if you

44

want to know the genuine history,'

'The history she doesn't know?' asked Patterson.

'She may well know it. I don't know. I know the history. It comes from a third century book written in Sanskrit. Hard to translate. But the book's entitled *"The Final*. That's probably the best way of describing it. And there's only a handful of pages remaining of it. Certainly, the original book. There's been some translations down the ages.'

'What does it say about the diamond?' asked Clarissa.

'The diamond is the key to a long-lost dwelling, wherein, the end times will be avoided on the road to paradise.'

Patterson nearly spat out his champagne. 'Excuse me,' he said. 'Did you get that from a fantasy novel?'

'Where do you think novels get their ideas from?' asked Farrier. 'This is from a book of the third century. And rather like the Templars, people who followed the teachings of the time may have continued to follow the thread through until this day. There are lots of things in the shadows. What you don't see,' said Farrier, 'are people who genuinely know not to make a fuss. But they're there. Not everybody looks for the acquisition of wealth. Some look for the acquisition of things that can get you out of a nasty future. The Templars were looking for eternal life. Those regarding the book of *The Final* are looking for a way out. And the Esoteric Tear is part of the machinery to achieve that.'

'Okay,' said Clarissa. 'Any names associated with it?'

'No. But you might find a later copy of the book. I believe the British Library has one in its collection. Not generally easy to get access to, but I guess as a police officer, you can manage it.'

Calissa drank the rest of her champagne, stood up and shook

hands with Farrier. 'Thank you, Edmund,' she said. Patterson shook hands as well, but his eyes were sceptical.

'Teach the boy well,' said Edmund, as Clarissa left. 'Make sure he understands things don't have to be real to be believed.'

'I tried to tell the boss that once.'

Soon they were walking along the south bank, a grey sky above them, with the odd break of sunshine. Clarissa pulled Patterson to one side, leaning her elbows on the wall as she stared out at the river.

'Listen, I'll say this once. You may think that man's off his rocker. You may think that the tale in the book is a load of nonsense. It may well be. But what you have to understand is not whether it's right or wrong. What you have to understand is whether people will believe that tale. And they will do so, either, A, to pay money for the diamond, or B, to acquire it. And if they believe that tale, they become very, very dangerous people.'

'Do you believe the tale?'

'Absolutely not,' said Clarissa, 'though I don't know it fully yet. But what I do know and fully believe, is that somebody grabbed that diamond for a reason. We need to dig out what's going on behind it. Where there's money, there are societies. Where there are societies, there's cover-ups. There are initiations. There are always people who believe they know more than everyone else and have the money to do daft things with it. This little baby, this little diamond, will cause great suffering,' said Clarissa. 'I can feel it in my bones already.'

She shook her head at the river flowing by. 'I never know why people just can't look at bloody art. They always have to make an arse of it.'

Chapter 06

Clarissa huffed and pulled the shawl around her as she walked out of the underground station. Up ahead of her, Patterson took in the air, looking round the London street.

'This way,' he said.

'Just you wait, Pats,' said Clarissa. 'There's a few more miles on these legs than there are on yours.'

She fought her way up the stairs, out into the street, and took a deep breath. It wasn't the most pleasant of breaths. She'd rather have been out in some country estate. Instead, she could smell the fumes from the traffic.

'When we get inside, I'm sitting down and I'm having a coffee first,' she said to Patterson. 'Then . . . actually, no; while I do that, you can find a librarian who can help us.'

'Don't I get a coffee?' asked Patterson.

'Do you want a coffee?'

'No,' said Patterson. 'I just thought it was unfair.'

Clarissa shook her head and marched past him. 'You definitely don't get a coffee now.'

Clarissa walked on, then stopped, realising that Patterson was the one who knew the way. He overtook her, and this time she fought hard not to fall behind. He would need to understand that she was a lady, and as one, he should afford her the privilege of commanding the pace. She marched on after him.

Entering the library, she searched desperately for somewhere to get a coffee. Spotting one, she sent Patterson on his way whilst she collapsed into a chair. Realising no one was going to come to serve her, she got up to the self-service counter and brought a coffee back, collapsing again.

She picked up her phone and made a brief phone call to Frank, her husband. He was working up at the club, out and currently on the second hole, but he seemed all right. He asked her was she okay, for she must have been panting. She told him once the coffee was in, she'd be fine. Patterson returned after ten minutes, insisting that Clarissa should follow him. She downed her coffee and took a short walk through the library, off to a private area, where they were welcomed by a librarian.

'Hello,' said the man. 'My name's Barnes, and I'm here to help you look for a book, Sergeant.'

'Detective Inspector Clarissa Urquhart.' Clarissa put her hand forward, shaking the man's, before pointing to her colleague. 'And this is Detective Constable Eric Patterson. Has Eric spoken to you about what we're looking for?'

'Yes, and I've sent for one of my colleagues. He said you're looking for a book called *The Final*. Although that's not its original name. He said it was possibly Sanskrit. It's not really my area of expertise. So, I've sent a runner off into the depths where we keep these sorts of people. And my colleague will be out soon.'

Clarissa thanked the man and then an awkward silence occurred while everyone stood around.

'Perhaps it would be better if we had somewhere to sit,' said Clarissa.

'I was kind of hoping my colleague would be here. They may want to take you further into the library, up to their own office. Sometimes some of the information is kept quite close to us, especially if that's the type of work we're looking at.'

'Does your colleague do a lot of this type of work?'

'In terms of cataloguing, knowing where various copies came from, yes. We're not doing anything with the interior of the book. We're librarians, here to catalogue, finding out the history of the books. Make sure they're in an available place for the public or indeed any specialist needs.'

Clarissa nodded and continued to stand. Five minutes later, a young woman appeared, maybe in her mid-twenties. She was tall, and possibly of Middle Eastern descent. Her skin was dark, a deep brown, and Clarissa thought she was rather elegant. She had a straight back. She was also thin, but in saying that, looked in the prime of life. Her nose was also narrow. Of course, Clarissa could tell she wasn't wearing any make-up.

'Hello,' said the woman, sporting a rather brutal southern English accent. 'My name's Clara. You're here looking for *The Final*, as they call it?'

'Yes,' said Clarissa. 'Would you have a copy?'

'Well, as you probably know, it's a third-century book. The original was in Sanskrit and, no, we don't have that. There is a believed copy in the rare books section. I'll find it. Perhaps you'd like to come with me. We'll go somewhere where we can look at it properly.'

She nodded to her colleague, turned, walked off, clearly believing that Clarissa and Patterson were going to follow.

49

They did so. After climbing a couple of flights of stairs, they were led into a room where they sat beside a table.

'I'll be back momentarily,' said the woman. 'I'll ask that you don't touch the copy when I bring it in.'

'Of course not,' said Clarissa; 'we're in your hands. We just need to know some information about it.'

Clarissa waited inside the room, wondering what to do. She turned to look out the window, but her current position meant she could only see the sky. She turned to Patterson. 'Do you think this is going to be any use?'

'I'm not an arts expert,' said Patterson.

'Well, you'll have to become one. What else do we need to ask this woman?'

'We need to ask Clara,' said Patterson, 'whether anyone else has requested to look at the copy.'

'Indeed.'

Clarissa sat, staring straight ahead, running through in her head what she wanted to ask and just how to deliver it. Suddenly, Clara burst into the room. She was holding some papers. In fact, she was holding a book underneath an arm. She set down a small volume and suddenly opened it. She was wearing gloves so as not to damage the copy.

'Somebody's been into this,' she blurted. 'Look!' She opened to about three or four pages in and there were ripped pages.

'When did that happen?' asked Clarissa.

'I don't know. This hasn't been brought out in nearly a year. And back then, it was fine. I know. I catalogued it.'

'So, nobody's come in and officially looked at it.'

'No. But somebody's come in and ripped this.'

'Is it locked away?' asked Clarissa.

'Oh yes. I mean, library staff can get it in and out, but this is quite disconcerting. Why would anyone want to look into this book? I mean, it's not valuable. You're not going to sell the pages.'

'The contents, how much do you know about them?' asked Clarissa.

'Not very much. This particular copy was acquired by the library almost thirty years ago. It's a translation, of course—actually a translation of a translation of a translation. And really, while it's kept in the rare books section, it's not worth that much.'

'So, it's the content they were after. And you're absolutely sure nobody's gone in and taken it.'

'I know nobody's taken it out to look at. That's all recorded. The area where it's stored, however, library staff have access to that all the time. It's not an expensive copy; it's not one of the ultra-rare items.'

'If you'll excuse me,' said Clara suddenly. She closed the book and went to leave the room. 'I need to report this.'

Clarissa stood up. 'Well thank you for your help, and we'll find our own way out.' As they walked back down the stairs, out towards the more public areas of the library, Patterson seemed to be thoughtful.

'What's up,' asked Clarissa.

'Maybe we should do a normal search in the library, look up the Esoteric Tear, find out what we can about it.'

'Go on then,' said Clarissa. 'You go ahead. You seem to know how these places work better than I do.'

'Are you going for another coffee?'

'I'm going to answer this phone,' said Clarissa, feeling that her mobile was vibrating inside of her shawl. She reached in and saw the name Macleod.

'It's the boss,' said Clarissa. 'I'd better answer it. Go on, go see what you can find. I'll look for you when I'm done.' She raised the phone to her ear. 'This is Clarissa.'

'Seoras here. They've been all up and down that loch. They haven't found the gem. The Esoteric Tear is still missing,' said Macleod. 'I put a lot of resources into finding that, but it's a non-starter.'

'So, I'm right,' said Clarissa.

'No, we haven't found the gem. Until you find it, you're not sure you're right. It could still be lost down there. Searching's not a—'

'Don't tell me it's not an exact science. You know I'm right, Seoras,' said Clarissa. 'It's all right; we've justified the trip.'

'And what have you learnt?'

'Well,' said Clarissa. 'The backstory to this particular gem, it's weird and fantastical, but it's one that certain people might invest in.'

'Like people with money. Maybe hedge funds, maybe . . .'

'No, no, no,' said Clarissa. 'Not like that. People who believe in these myths and legends, people who are tied into it. You ever heard of the Templars?'

'Of course,' said Macleod. 'These people are the Templars?'

'No, they're not the Templars. But alchemy was big in its day, possibly still is according to some people, eternal life, things like that. There are societies who will go for things that indicate such. This gemstone is believed to open a portal to keep you safe during the end times. You know, Armageddon.'

'And what, somebody's nicking it for that.'

'You don't have to believe it,' said Clarissa. 'In this world I inhabit, things take on value for various reasons. Some because of the way they look; some people have a love of beauty or quality. Other people have a love of investment, knowing an item will increase in value. This item isn't like that. This item is believed to do something that makes it command a price. A price that the people who really have money can afford.'

'You talked to Ali Ralston, didn't you? I thought she told you it wasn't worth much.'

'In the normal world, it's not. But if somebody wants something bad enough, they'll pay whatever to get it.'

'How are you going to track it down?' asked Macleod.

'Over here at the British Library, there's a book about it. It tells you the story, all about it. I have been quite disturbed to find out that some pages have been ripped out of it. Somebody's on the trail of this gem for what it does. That's quite clear. We just need to find out where to look next.'

'Now don't spend too long down there. I can't afford to stand you for that amount of money. It's not a murder inquiry we're on?'

'Oh, thanks for reminding me.'

'How's Patterson getting on—now he's back in the field?'

'Pats is fine. Absolutely fine,' said Clarissa. 'I've got to get on. I'll call you later.'

She closed down the call and wandered through the British Library, looking for Patterson. She eventually found him at a reading desk, in front of him, a small tome.

'Are you enjoying yourself?' asked Clarissa, marching up behind him.

'This book—I think it might be useful,' said Patterson.

'Why? Who's it by?'

'Reginald McLean,' said Patterson. 'You won't have heard of him. He lives in Edinburgh. I did a search and we wouldn't have found this in the older days. But because you can reference things a lot more, I tagged up the keyword, *The Final*. Reg McLean is someone who was into all of that lore and may help us.'

'What, he wrote a book on it?'

'He did indeed. I've been looking it up on the internet. And it seems that he didn't get that many copies published. It was removed from sale quickly. He deposited some copies in the British library, as you're meant to do when you produce a book. Which is lucky for us because I've found him up in Edinburgh.'

'Okay' said Clarissa. 'That's one line to go down. However, I think we need to look at the other side of this. Macleod says they couldn't find the gemstone in the loch. So, I believe my assertion that the gem was taken, and the rest dumped, is correct. Somebody's got to handle it. I'm going to talk to some dealers who could do this and do it on the quiet. Find out if there's any noise about it.'

'So, I'll go up to Edinburgh on my own,' said Patterson.

'Yes,' said Clarissa. 'You're good with that, aren't you? I mean, what's going to happen? You're going off to interview an old man. We're on the Arts team now,' said Clarissa. 'Really bad things don't happen. Well, they do, but they tend to be a priceless painting getting slashed. You drop the vase.

'People don't end up dead on the Arts team. So, you get yourself up there. Find out what this Reginald can tell us. See if you can get any names of people associated with it. We need to get inside this society. Find out who wants it. Who, in their right mind, would go to all this trouble. And I'll find out who could do it for them.'

Patterson nodded and closed up the volume before returning it back to the library. Soon, they were making their way back on the underground to the hotel they'd stayed at. She'd need to get a car, for she'd left the little green one up the road. It was quicker to fly. But now she was going to have to whiz around parts of the country and Clarissa was annoyed that her car was left up north.

Still, this was better. Better than a murder investigation. This case had no dead bodies to look at. She'd swished it up in London and next she'd be racing off to who knows where. Wales, she thought. That's the first one to try. Wales.

Chapter 07

Patterson stepped off the plane at Edinburgh Airport and adjusted his cravat. He had over his shoulder a small bag carrying the necessaries that he had taken to London. He walked out through the terminal towards the car hire desk to pick up one he'd reserved earlier. In truth, he was enjoying the travel.

Clarissa Urquhart was a strange boss. She was a woman he owed his life to, and she seemed to have his best interests at heart. Patterson liked everything to be done properly. He liked to treat people in a professional and civil manner. She was from an older school. Someone who liked to get stuck in, rattle a few cages.

She had been right, though, about the gem. And he was convinced that it was now in circulation somewhere. Someone had it. Someone was looking for it. As he signed for the car hire, Patterson collected the keys and turned to see two men on the far side of the concourse. One looked away quickly, while one stared at him. It unnerved Patterson. And, most instinctively, he reached up and touched his cravat.

It was in the way of what he really wanted to touch. His throat. Everyone always thought you were healed. You just got over it. You worked away to get on with life and you put to bed what had happened.

He hadn't. He still saw it in his nightmare sometimes. Patterson could still feel that knife cutting through his neck, but he had a second chance now. So, he would not complain.

He looked over at the man who had been staring at him, but he was looking away now. Patterson wondered if this was all part of the recovery. The people who had done this to him were not good people, and it had taken him a while to get back out into the field. Clarissa clearly thought he was ready for it. For here she was, sending him on his own up to Edinburgh.

He'd interview Reginald McLean. But as Clarissa had said, he was going to interview an old man, and they would talk a lot about fantastical history. It wasn't like he was going to interview a murderer. He wasn't walking into the lion's den of a load of terrorists. He was going to interview an old man who wrote a book that sold little. All about a gemstone that wasn't worth that much, but yet people were probably after. How bad could it get?

Patterson smiled and thought about grabbing a coffee on the way out. But no, get on, get business done, then sit down and have your coffee. Patterson wasn't that au fait with Edinburgh, but the sat-nav took him to the bottom of a block of flats. There were several here, all within reach of each other, but Patterson found his block and began what turned out to be a long climb to the top floor.

The lift wasn't working, but rather than curse, Patterson took it as a chance to exercise. Everyone needed exercise, after all. It was good for the mind, and his mind needed clearing out every day. That's what the therapist said: every day do your processes, go through the things that you do to get yourself in the position that you want to be in, and you'll be okay.

He followed these processes he'd learnt; he'd gone back into the station room, he'd got on, even with the murder team, though he wasn't working out of the office with them. Patterson was meant to be out there but he'd done the paperwork, and in Clarissa, he'd been given an opportunity.

Arts couldn't be any worse, could they? Theft, after all, wasn't murder. It was bound to be, maybe, even more glamorous.

Patterson had found the classical station in the car as he'd driven over. Finding it early had calmed him, so that now, by the time he'd reached the top floor of the block of flats, he was in a good frame of mind. He confidently walked up and rapped on the door.

There was no doorbell. There was no number. It was the top flat, and he'd just assumed. The door opposite said 'cleaner'. The door opened and facing Patterson was a man in his eighties, with grey hair, who looked rather unsteady on his feet.

'Yeah,' said the man.

'My name's Detective Constable Eric Patterson. I work for Police Scotland and I'd like to talk to you about a book you wrote.'

'All the bills were paid on that. I know I didn't make any money. I know it.'

'I'm not here because you've done anything wrong. I'm here because I believe you can help us understand.'

'Understand what?' asked the man. He was half behind the door, peering at Patterson, one eye slightly more dominant than the other.

'With regards to a book called *The Final*,"' said Patterson. The man almost sprang forward. He looked around behind Patterson before waving him inside. Patterson stepped through, turned, and watched the man close the door behind him with four different locks.

'Are you scared of something? It is Mr McLean, isn't it?'

'Reginald McLean. Yes, I fear something.'

'What?'

'You clearly don't know enough about *The Final*.' You don't know about the secret societies behind it. Why are you looking into it?'

The man brushed past Patterson, who followed him into a small lounge. Reginald sat down on a sofa, his back to a large window, through which Patterson could see the top floor of another block of flats. Sitting down opposite but at a slightly acute angle to him, Patterson took out his notebook.

'We're hunting the Esoteric Tear,' said Patterson.

'What? Who are you?' said the man. 'Police don't follow things like that.'

Reaching inside his jacket, Patterson took out his warrant card and placed it in front of the man. 'I am DC Eric Patterson. We're hunting the Esoteric Tear because it's been stolen. There was a display of it, and other gemstones, at Urquhart Castle on the side of Loch Ness. From there it was stolen. We recovered the other gems, but the Tear . . .'

'The Tear is missing? The Tear is out there. So, there's no—they'll all be going for it. All of them.'

'Who?' asked Patterson.

'Both sides.'

'Sides? Slow down a minute,' said Patterson. 'You need to tell me what's going on.'

The man stood up for a moment, shook his head, walked

59

off to one side of the room, and then turned and peered at Patterson. 'Are you sure you're polis?'

'I'm sure. My warrant card says, I'm sure. If you want, you can ring the station.'

'Which station?'

It suddenly dawned on Patterson his answer may not satisfy the man as much as he hoped. 'Inverness Station.'

'Why Inverness Station? What are you doing down here?'

'I work with the Arts team. We're spread all over the country. Please ring the station. I won't give you the number. If you find the number, ring it. Remember, I'm the Arts section, so ask for someone in the Arts section.'

The man nodded and pulled out what looked like a small iPad. He tapped some things into it. Then he picked up his phone, dialled and waited until someone answered on the other end. There then began a conversation between him and a person who was presumably the desk sergeant. And then there was a rather gruff and short conversation before the man put the phone down and sat back down on the sofa.

'Your Chief Detective Inspector Macleod says you're genuine. I know Macleod, I've seen him on the telly. But he's not Arts, he's—'

'He's both at the moment. He's the man at the top of my particular section. But his main thing is running the murder squads,' said Patterson.

'What do you know about the Esoteric Tear?' asked Reginald.

'It's a diamond; it's not actually worth a lot; it's talked about in a book called *The Final*. *The Final* was originally in Sanskrit, and we found a copy in the British Library with pages ripped out.' Reginald's face became even more worried. 'And that's about it really . . . oh, and it's missing,'

'You know so very little,' said Reginald, 'people who've studied *The Final* have been looking for the Esoteric Tear all over Europe. The Templars looked at it but they didn't believe in it but other people did. The background is such an old religion, and the Tear has been around for a long time. It disappeared for about five hundred years, then came back up and disappeared again. Most recently, it was gained by Scottish museums.

'They, of course, don't believe any of the story, but the societies that sought it have continued on and on through the years. They fought over it. Some wanted to control it. Some saw it as a good thing. Others wanted to visit a vengeance on what we were doing. Many say it's tied into the environmental lobby . . .'

'Excuse me,' said Patterson. The man seemed to be rambling on a bit and it was quite hard to get an idea of the full story. 'These people, these modern-day people, because that's who's going to have taken it, isn't it? You said there's two sides.'

'Yes, all devout believers. The mainstay of it is in Scotland at the moment. There are a few lords and people high in society, but they have their runners.'

'How do they meet?' asked Patterson. 'Who are they?'

'They meet in quiet places, like all societies. Most of them masked—half of them don't know each other. And the names, well, that was what happened with the book. When I originally wrote the book, I had names in and they got taken out. They came to see me, came to visit, and they said they'd monitor me always, always be there to check on me.'

'Who,' asked Patterson.

'The societies, the organisation, didn't I tell you? The Dwellers, although that's not correct; the original's in Sanskrit

61

here.'

He reached over and grabbed a pencil and piece of paper and wrote a name in Sanskrit. To Patterson, it looked like a lot of different symbols he didn't understand.

'The book also calls them inhabitants, people who stay inside—those who will be safe when the apocalypse comes.'

'I'm having a hard time at the moment,' said Patterson, 'getting on with all this mythology. As an officer, I need to know who's following this, or who may be on the trail of our gemstone. So, I'd really like some names, some people I can go to, people I can—'

'But you won't tell them they come from me, will you?'

'No, if that's an issue.'

'It's not an issue,' said the man. 'It's my life. I was lucky last time. They let me live. And look at me. Look where I am now.'

Patterson looked around him. The man's flat looked decrepit. It had lots of what Patterson would describe as knick-knacks, although they were more of a religious nature. At least, they seemed to have an intentional use. They weren't dog and cat ornaments, but rather, shapes and mystic symbols.

'I'm sure we can protect you,' said Patterson, 'if that's the case. If you really think there's a threat to you, we can take you into safe houses, safe places.'

'But they're throughout society,' said Reginald. 'You don't understand. You don't know how big this is.'

'Well, give me some names then,' said Patterson. 'Give me some names and I'll understand.'

'Well, up in Scotland,' said Reginald, 'and you have to promise me you won't tell anyone this, but up in Scotland there's a secret—'

It all happened so fast. Patterson didn't flinch. There was a crash as the window of the flat blew out. Almost at the same time, McLean's head half exploded at the back. Blood whipped across the room, splattering Patterson. As he half moved away, the body of Reginald McLean pitched forward, off the sofa, hitting a small table in front of him, then collapsing to one side.

Patterson, whose eyes were blinking because of the blood splatter across his face, hit the floor, and could feel himself beginning to shake. His body rippled with shock. He went to stand back up but stopped himself.

Think, he told himself, *think, Patterson, what are you doing? Don't do something reckless. There's a gunman, a gunman up there. You need to get to the door, you need to—no, ring it in, ring it in.*

He crawled his way right up to the wall where the window had been, with glass cutting into his hands as he moved across. Small trickles of blood ran from them. He pulled out his phone, dialling 999. He felt he shouted what was going on. Patterson felt he didn't deliver it in the correct way. But as they told him, they were on their way. His hands began to shake.

This was the art world, thought Patterson. *It isn't meant to happen like this. I'd left it behind. It wasn't meant to happen.* Slowly, he tried to regain composure.

Crawling round to the body of Reginald Mclean on the ground, he tried to check his pulse. When he saw that half the head at the back was missing, Patterson just rolled out of the way, over to a wall. He stayed there until there was a banging on the door. Carefully, he made his way across and unlocked the door. He manoeuvred himself to the outside, closing the door behind him.

Shakingly, he explained to his police colleagues what had happened. Several tore off to go to the next block of flats from where the shots had come. Things were happening, actions were being put into motion, but Patterson just sat on the floor. He was still shaking, still wondering what had happened. In his mind, he could feel a knife cutting deep into his neck.

Chapter 08

Clarissa Urquhart drove her hire car across the Severn Bridge, heading in towards Monmouth. She'd cut up from Chepstow to root in through the back roads before making her way to the small town on the Welsh border.

It was rather quaint in its own way, so very different from Newport. It had been a while since she'd passed through it. She only had a passing acquaintance with the town, nothing more, but she'd bought a few items there, back in her heyday. The woman she'd bought them off was Sheila Alcock.

Sheila was a dealer of precious goods, able to get you anything, especially the things that money couldn't buy. According to intelligence from the Arts team, Sheila had also been visited recently by several Arab buyers. One of them was Abbas Aboud, and he was known to have several links to some Scottish lords.

That was the joy of the art world. Often you were dealing with people who were high up, people of influence, people who had money. That or people who came from old money who had little money anymore. Such a mix. Clarissa loved it. She thrived on being in amongst it.

A woman like Sheila Alcock, Clarissa understood. Sheila

enjoyed the art that she sourced. She appreciated the items that she obtained for people, but behind it all, she was also a ruthless businesswoman. She merely used her own talent to get that which others sought after.

Sheila was a bad person according to the law, but really, she was like a modern-day tinker. She'd get hold of what others wanted and sell it on to them. She never gained things illegally herself. Somebody else always did that. She was just a connections person, a person who could verify items that came her way. Clarissa sometimes wondered if she could have ended up that way.

Yes, she understood Sheila Alcock, but Sheila must also be around the same age as Clarissa was. Time to hang up the boots. Time to just turn round and say, enough's enough, and go home. Surely, she must have had a nest egg.

She lived on a little farm, just on the edge of Monmouth. Well, she called it a farm. There were some chickens and she had pigs last time as well, if Clarissa remembered correctly. She wasn't sure what else was left. The farm seemed to grow and shrink every time Clarissa had gone past it. And in fairness, it had been a few years now, so she was unsure just what she was walking into.

The road up out of Monmouth into the hills had changed little. Large trees lined every side, and you couldn't see ahead of you more than maybe fifty to one hundred metres at a time as the road swung in and out and up towards the hills. It was as she swung around one of these bends that she turned onto a gravel track. The track headed off through a field, down past a small brook, over a bridge, and towards a building.

It was a small bungalow, not a farmhouse. Sheila had it built properly, knocking down the one that had been there before.

She said that had been an aberration. Of course, she had gone against the normal habit of people of her own ilk. They wanted to preserve the past.

Clarissa stepped out and looked over at the bungalow. The front door was open.

'Sheila' called Clarissa, 'you about?'

It wasn't unusual for Sheila not to be in the house. It was a farm, after all. Clarissa wandered round the near side of the building, down a small path to where the chicken enclosure had been last time. As she walked along, she heard a cockerel, and he came strutting towards her. Clarissa stopped, keeping a respectful distance. She'd be walking into his territory, so she shouted over the top of him.

'Sheila, you there? Sheila? It's Clarissa. I need to talk to you, Sheila.'

Sheila, of course, knew that Clarissa was now a police officer. She'd found out and blown Clarissa's cover during an arts festival, causing Clarissa to have to leg it. Clarissa had forgiven her. After all, Sheila was just doing her business.

Clarissa went to step forward, and the cockerel stamped his feet.

'Is she down there?' Clarissa said to the bird.

He didn't reply. Just stared. Beyond him, Clarissa could see the group of hens that were clearly his. Slowly, she backed away until the cockerel turned and made his way back towards his hen house.

Clarissa turned back and walked towards the bungalow, feeling a ray of sunshine on her face. London had been grey, but here were the country smells. There was manure on the fields, there was the babbling of the small brook, just down by the edge of the property. Clarissa had wandered round to the rear of the house where she saw some greenhouses and there was the small garage over at the side. She walked over, but the door was closed.

She tried it; it opened easily. Clarissa stepped inside to see an old Morris Minor. Clarissa loved sports cars, especially older looking sports cars. Sheila had just liked old cars. Clarissa remembered having a conversation with her about them and Sheila was indeed well versed in them. Clarissa wouldn't have a dowdy thing like this, though.

She turned and left the car behind in the garage and started walking back towards the house. Clarissa continued round the side of the bungalow that she hadn't been on, looking out to the fields and shouting for Sheila before she made it back to her own car.

She'd wait in the car for a bit. Maybe Sheila had gone for a walk. Clarissa didn't want to jump into the house. After all, Sheila could be involved, or maybe a suspect. She may be the fence they were going to use to move the item on. Clarissa couldn't just wander into her house. It might not help the investigation. She'd have to be a bit more formal as much as she didn't want to be.

Clarissa looked back towards the house one more time. Did something move in the window? Was that a figure? Clarissa looked again. It had been, hadn't it? Something had moved. It wasn't a trick of the light. The sun was in the wrong place to cause that.

Clarissa walked over, not creeping because she thought Sheila was maybe just hiding. She got to the front door and rapped on it, although it was open.

'Sheila Alcock. It's Clarissa Urquhart. We need to talk. Can you hear me? If you're in, I'd like you to come to the door.

Sheila, I'm not arresting you. I'm not here for something you've done. I need information. Only need—'

She thought you heard a noise inside. Had she?

There was something. A sound almost like a gurgle. Something was up. Something must be wrong. She'd heard a gurgle. Somebody might be in trouble.

Clarissa stepped inside, wondering where she'd heard it come from. She wandered through, down the central hallway, into the kitchen at the rear. She saw an aga at the centre of a perfectly old-styled kitchen. There were some rather ornate beams, that actually weren't of any age, for this was a relatively modern build. But they'd done it with older looking taste, which was nice.

Clarissa saw a cup of coffee. She passed her hand over the top. It was still warm. It didn't look warm, but felt warm enough. She walked through the kitchen to the dining room at the rear. But no one was there. It hadn't been set. There was no sign that anyone had been using it.

Clarissa made her way through to the front room. There was a sofa, and a television in the corner. There was also a photo of a local celebrity. Donny Hughes. She remembered him from the TV. He'd done those arts programmes where people where bidding or trying to sell their tat. *He was a right shyster*, she thought and grinned suddenly. But he was well liked, and he knew his stuff.

She laughed at it, wondering why Sheila had it. Did she know him better than that? Had she got to know him? Was this actually just celebrity worship?

She went to walk out of the room, and suddenly something dawned on Clarissa. The sofa. It was a sofa that was there the last time she'd dropped by. That was several years ago now.

The sofa was the same, but something about it wasn't right.

In the right-hand corner of the room was a table and last time the table had been locked in place, with the sofa on one side of a protruding edge and the chair on the other. The chair wasn't touching the edge of this table. The sofa had been pulled forward, so the chair and the sofa still created an L-shape that was perfect, but the sofa was off the wall. It had come forward by maybe a foot.

Why? There was no need. Was there something around the back? Clarissa turned, and walked back slowly. She peered down. As she peered round the corner of the sofa, someone jumped out from behind it, grabbing her by the throat.

Clarissa rocked, taking several steps backwards. The man came with force, but Clarissa managed to spin him, sending him crashing off towards the TV. He hit it with a thud; the TV rocked backwards. There was a loud smash, but the man came back towards Clarissa.

He was wearing a mask, but he had thick shoulders and powerful arms, as he again grabbed Clarissa by the throat. She put her hands up, trying to pry them off, but she couldn't do so, and was pushed backwards towards the small chair. Clarissa was pushed down into it, the man pressing hard with his thumbs on her throat. She felt herself beginning to choke, felt herself beginning to weaken. Her hands couldn't push him away. He was too strong. She'd have to do something; she'd have to do it quick.

Clarissa reached out with her right hand, fumbling on the table for anything. She found a vase and instantly brought it round, where it smashed hard over the man's head. He stumbled backwards, his hands instantly releasing from Clarissa. She swung again, catching him on the shoulder now, but this time the vase had been smashed, and the strike wasn't that strong.

She desperately looked for something else in case he retaliated. Sitting on the chair, she wondered if he'd jump back on top of her again, but he ran, disappearing out through the door of the living room and straight out the front door.

Clarissa hauled herself up, still gasping for breath. She got to the door and saw that the man was already halfway down the driveway. She wouldn't catch him. Doubled over, she breathed in hard, and then something struck her. Where was Sheila then?

She rewound her path through the house, realising that Sheila wasn't in any of the rooms she'd gone to so far. Clarissa walked over and checked the cupboard under the stairs, Sheila wasn't there, so she checked the other downstairs room, no Sheila. She walked to a back bedroom and found it immaculate, pristine and completely empty. As she got to the next one along, something was bothering her. Was that a gurgle?

Clarissa opened the door. Lying on the bed, a pool of blood around her, was Sheila Alcock. She wasn't moving much; the body, though, was still going through its death throes. Clarissa picked up her phone, dialled, and placed it on the speaker setting so she could talk whilst she worked on Sheila Alcock. She looked down and saw the slice across the throat. Her mind reeled; just like Patterson. Her hands shook. She put her hands across Sheila's throat, the blood staining them. It was happening again, all over again.

'Which service do you require?'

'Ambulance,' said Clarissa. She put her hand down and couldn't feel her chest rising and falling. There was no pulse when she checked it.

71

So, the conversation began, but Clarissa knew it was too late. There was no pulse and though she continued CPR, the throat had been cut. There was nothing. The occasional gurgle, the occasional body spasm. But no life was coming back.

Unlike Patterson, whose heart had still been beating, and who had still been breathing, Shelia was gone. Clarissa had clung on to Patterson's throat and kept it functional. But Sheila was gone. Clarissa stepped away when the ambulance crew ran in. She took herself out into the hallway of the house and collapsed, sitting down.

Taking out her phone, Clarissa put it on the ground, and pressed for a call to Macleod. She put it on speaker, as he picked up at the other end.

'It's Seoras. Are you okay?'

She didn't speak, but the sobbing tears she cried must have told him everything.

Chapter 09

Clarissa was sitting in front of her laptop in her hotel room, not quite fully recovered from the incident earlier on in the day. She was waiting patiently by the screen, but was getting frustrated at Macleod still trying to connect through. She imagined Als in the background, sorting the man out before disappearing quietly out of his office. Als would then stand around outside for a couple of minutes.

Patterson was already on, and from what Clarissa could see on the screen, he looked gaunt. No wonder. She had said to him that there was no way something so dark could happen again, as had happened to them on the murder team. Sitting across from someone whose brain got blown out in front of you was probably akin to having your own throat slashed. She would have to talk to Seoras about how they would look after Patterson from this one. *On the bright side*, she thought, *he's already in counselling. I don't have to set that up.*

There was another person on the call. DS Sabine Ferguson, a colleague Clarissa had met only once. She'd been introduced to her as part of the Arts team and was working out of the Glasgow office. Clarissa remembered that first meeting.

Sabine Ferguson was tall, blonde-haired, with a distinct

German look. However, when she spoke, she had a thick Northern Irish accent. Part Austrian, part Irish, she said, which made Clarissa realise she couldn't tell the difference between a German and an Austrian accent. It was something she was going to have to work on. She imagined if somebody called her English, she would do her lid. She was thankful that she hadn't called Ferguson German.

The Arts team in Glasgow was small, only two members there, and currently the other was on holiday. So, Ferguson was joining in, now that the case was taking on arms and legs.

'Is that it? Am I going through now, Ross?'

Clarissa rolled her eyes. Every time with Macleod! He just didn't get the technology these days and struggled badly.

'We're hearing you,' said Patterson. 'I'm getting you loud and clear, Seoras.'

'Well, now that the elderly and infirm have joined us, can we make a start?' asked Clarissa.

She saw the rather nervous face of Sabine Ferguson and Patterson's rather doubtful look at the comment. But Macleod simply gave her a cheeky smile.

'I don't think there's that many years between us,' he said.

'No, but some of us have lasted better,' said Clarissa. 'Can we get on?'

'Of course,' said Macleod. 'First off, rough day, everyone. Rough day all round. Are we okay? Does anybody . . .'

Clarissa waited, wanting Patterson to respond first. She was fine, but she didn't want to say that, and push the man into a similar response. What he had suffered was far worse. Clarissa was never bothered by what happened to her. She was always more bothered by what happened to other people.

Seeing a dead child in the course of a murder investigation

74

had nearly torn her apart. Seeing what happened to Patterson *had* torn her apart. She had rescued him, she had saved him, and yet she thought she had seen a part of him die, because he wasn't the same man coming out on the other side. Maybe part of what she was doing was to bring him to that place, to be himself again. And now this was a further setback.

'I won't lie to you,' said Patterson. 'It's been pretty rough. I phoned the counsellor before this call. We were on the phone for an hour. He thinks I'm okay to continue, and I'd like to continue.'

'Do you think you're okay?' asked Clarissa.

'I believe so, but I wanted to get him to check me though, too.'

'What about yourself?' said Macleod. He clearly thought he was looking at Clarissa, not getting the idea that you were simply looking out of a screen. Depending where the other person was, your eyes weren't necessarily on them.

She ignored this and simply gave a curt, 'Of course.'

'I just want to say a hello as well to Sabine joining us,' said Macleod. 'I've not really worked with you before but it's good to have you on the team. This case has taken on rather more than was first thought. I'm interested in getting an extensive investigation together. I've asked for assistance from Uniform up here in Inverness, and down in Glasgow if you need it, Sabine. We need to be careful because we've now got a murder investigation running, too.'

'Can I say something about that?' asked Clarissa.

'Of course,' said Macleod.

'Let the murder investigation run. I think this was a hitman and *we* won't find him. This team won't find a hitman. The murder team may, and they may be able to follow back to who sent him. I think we may need to use other lines of attack to find that person, and to see the core of this. So, bring the murder team on, Seoras. You liaise with them and let us run this through purely as a robbery investigation.'

'It'll be two murders though,' said Macleod, 'one of which is down in Wales. I'll end up with two teams running it.'

'You're big enough and bright enough,' said Clarissa. Macleod lifted his eyebrows at her and then put them back down.

'I wasn't questioning my competence,' said Macleod, 'but I'm delighted you have faith in me. I understand where you're coming from and with such a small team, maybe we can solve this on an arts train of thought. Thinking of the murder side, I could bring in Hope to assist on the murders.'

'You've got people in Glasgow,' said Clarissa, 'and we've got people in Wales. Let them do it. They'll be very detached from us. Then they'll be reporting to you in a very unbiased level. Don't bring the Inverness team in.'

'I take it this isn't just you trying to flex your own wings. Make sure you're not stepped upon by people who are above you.'

'The only person above me is you,' said Clarissa, 'and frankly, I've just dumped a complete load of work on you. So, I think I'm doing pretty well on that front. Let me get on with this. The art world is different, Seoras. You need to understand it. You need to see through the black and white, see the areas of grey. Spot the people who are, well, maybe not squeaky clean but decent, spot the ones who unashamedly aren't. It's not always that easy, and it's not—'

'Can we stop the lecture?' said Macleod. 'I've said yes. So, what's your line of attack from a purely arts point of view?'

She had been lecturing him, and she probably deserved that. Macleod had given her a lot of latitude and he never reacted to the way she spoke to him in front of others, especially the team. But she had just dumped a load of work on him. He was going to be working hard, coordinating, and now she was going to dump something else on him, too.

'Well, as I see it, we don't have a lot to go on.'

'As I see it,' said Macleod, 'I think we've got quite a bit to go on, even if you ignore the murders. Let's look at the Aboud link. Abbas Aboud is known to have been in Wales at Sheila Alcock's. Several other buyers went to visit her. Abbas Aboud was one of them. Suddenly she's dead. We need to chase down the Aboud link. Intelligence from the arts world says that he has links to several Scottish lords. Meanwhile,' said Macleod, 'Patterson said he was seconds from the names of the Dwellers, the group that apparently wants this Esoteric Tear. That's the second play. Get through that, find names. Chase it through. Somebody didn't want Reginald speaking. Now he's dead.

'I wouldn't be surprised if the flat wasn't bugged,' said Macleod. 'They're looking at the flat, of course, but it would make sense if they could hear. After all, they killed him just before he was about to let out significant names.'

'He had been warned off with the book,' said Clarissa.

'That's right,' said Patterson. 'He seemed extremely nervous when I spoke to him about it. He seemed to be very wary. It was like they'd kept a check on him, almost as if he was dead. Was as if he knew for he was very frightened.'

Macleod went silent. Patterson was not looking at the screen but looking down towards his feet.

'You okay, Pats?' said Clarissa.

"Pats!" said Macleod. "Seriously? You're calling him Pats?"

'Yes?' said Clarissa. 'Pats.'

'You still have Als working with me. Now I've got Pats. Just don't call me Mac," said Macleod. "Pats indeed."

"You're aware I'm on the call?" said Patterson suddenly.

"Yes, of course we are. Anything else to add, Pats?' said Clarissa. Macleod had done it deliberately, she was sure, to give Pats a jolt out of his sombre thoughts.

'I think the Chief Inspector's right. I think we're going to need to look at the Dwellers. See if we can get the names. Seems to me the Aboud link is solid enough, but it could be about something completely different. He could have been chasing Sheila Alcock for something else. It could be a case also that she's done the dirty on something else, and that's what's cost her.'

'Except for the fact,' said Macleod, 'that we know the Esoteric Tear is missing, and she's someone with the ability to ship it on.'

'But it's not an Arab thing, is it?' said Patterson.

'If you don't mind me butting in,' said Sabine, springing to life suddenly, 'I think all of these lines of inquiry stand up. So, let's just get on and inquire about them. I'm down in Glasgow at the moment. As I understand it, Eric's over there in Edinburgh. Clarissa's down in Wales. Maybe we should look at teaming up, especially with the potential threat that now is out there. After all, we have two dead on our hands.'

'You're absolutely right,' said Macleod. 'Well, Clarissa,' he said, 'you're the DI; it's your investigation. Tell me what you want.'

'Okay, Pats and I will try to find out more about the Dwellers down south. I'll come up and join him towards Edinburgh. Sabine, you head up to Inverness and join up with the boss.

There's a list of lords that Aboud was attached to. I suggest you interview them all. It'll be good having you there, anyway. Seoras, the bigwig; a lot of them like that. And a smart woman. Sabine's better on the eyes than me as well.'

'So what? You're sending up the trumped-up boss along with the good-looking one,' said Macleod.

'Well, some people just aren't ready for me,' said Clarissa, laughing. 'And anyway, Pats got on to this Dwellers idea. He's in with the whole mythology so he needs to be doing that and I need to get myself back up the road and to pick my car up at some point.'

'I'll see if there's anybody heading down to the Glasgow-Edinburgh region,' said Macleod. 'Let them drive it down for you.'

'I want their names before they get in that car,' said Clarissa.

'Look, I paid for the thing to come back from what was basically the dead in car terms,' said Macleod. 'I will not let just anyone in it.'

'Fine, but I'll hold you responsible,' said Clarissa.

'Right, that's all done then,' said Macleod. 'Sabine, get yourself up here for the morning and we'll head out. Clarissa, get on the move. I'll see if I can get your car down to you for tomorrow. Patterson, take the rest of the night off. Feet up, relax, do something. Talk to your counsellor if you need to. You've not had a good one. I think it's important that we all make sure we're all right before we leap back into it.'

Patterson nodded, and closed down the call, followed by Sabine. But before Macleod went, Clarissa shouted to him through the call.

'I'm only on this side,' said Macleod. 'I'm not deaf.'

'Sorry. Technology, eh? Look, I think we need to get

79

somebody else on to Pats. That sort of thing just unnerves you, Seoras. I mean, have you seen somebody die in front of you like that?'

'I've actually seen a few things,' said Macleod, 'but not quite that one. But he seems good. He's been checked out by his counsellor. I think he's okay to go. And besides, you're going to be with him. You'll be more sensitive to that than I will.'

'No, I won't. I know what you're like. You look after the team. I'll do it too. I'll make sure he's okay.'

'Well, I'm going to get off. I've got to check in with the murder squad,' said Macleod, 'and then get to bed. Tell Jane that you're sending me out with another woman from far off to investigate things.'

'You're going to have to watch yourself. I mean Sabine. Tall, slender, good looking. You're going to get a reputation.'

'And you're the one giving it to me. But it's all right. I'll just tell them I'll send you next time.'

Clarissa laughed. She went to close the call, but Macleod put his hand up to the screen.

'What?' she asked. 'What's that mean?'

'I didn't want to shout,' he said. 'Are you okay? Patterson's one thing. If he's not okay, we'll stand him down. We'll bring in somebody else. Not a problem. But you're running the investigation. When you said you were okay, are you okay?'

'How long have you got? It's over,' said Clarissa.

'I've got as long as it takes,' said Macleod.

Clarissa took a deep breath. She looked up and saw a face that was usually so serious, flooded with concern. She felt her eyes well up.

'I thought it was Patterson all over again. I looked and saw her throat,' said Clarissa, beginning to choke. 'And I saw

Patterson. My hand, and the blood, and the—' suddenly the dam broke, and she cried.

'It's okay,' said Macleod. 'Let it go. Just let it go.'

Chapter 10

Clarissa stepped out of her hotel the following morning, embracing what was clean, fresh country air. She actually liked this part of the world. It was barely inland and there were plenty of rolling fields, animals about, less of the big city. She really was a country girl at heart. The reason she loved her golf was because it got her out in the open air.

Macleod had rung sometime earlier and advised that her car was on its way down and would be dropped off at Glasgow Police Station. Clarissa was delighted, but she'd still have to drive the other hire vehicle for a while, a prospect she wasn't looking forward to.

The seat just didn't sit right. You couldn't get comfortable. And at the end of the day, there was no hood. You couldn't pull it down and let the wind go through your hair. There was no zip when you put the foot to the floor. It was not her green sports car. But then, not much ever could be.

As she took a stroll into town and sat down for a coffee at a local coffee shop, Clarissa answered her vibrating mobile.

'This is DCI Urquhart. Who's speaking?'

'It's Detective Sergeant Raleigh. Yeah, I know, I know. Yeah, like the bike. But listen; we've been searching the flat of Reginald McLean and we've discovered some correspondence from, we believe, what was his editor for one of his books? I think it was the book that your constable was talking to him about. The editor's name's Lynn Green and she lives in Gairlochy. The correspondence is pretty bland. Just asking when his next chapters were going to arrive. But I thought that address might be useful to you.'

'Thank you. I'll head over and talk to her.'

'We also thought that maybe she might be in danger.'

'Anything else in the house to say who she was?' asked Clarissa.

'I don't believe so. As far as we can tell, most of it is actually about the contents of the book. There're bits and pieces stuck up on the wall. I've tried getting one of our constables to read through them and to read through whatever we can find of the book. I'll send it all through to you.'

'Send it all through to Patterson. He's covering off that side for me,' said Clarissa. 'And thank you. That's given us somewhere to go.'

Clarissa closed the call, picked up her coffee, and placed a call to Patterson.

'How are we doing?' asked Patterson, rather forced.

'How am I doing? What about yourself?'

'I'm holding up. I had a few nightmares last night. Can't say I'm in the best of condition, but I'm functional.'

'Good,' said Clarissa. She didn't want to challenge his belief, didn't want him to think that he wasn't okay, if indeed he was. The man's confidence must have been shot through at this point. She needed to make sure that it stayed as high as it could.

'I've been speaking to the Edinburgh police. They've fired through an address. Well, more of a location. Gairlochy for a Lynn Green.'

'Lynn Green?'

'Yes, his editor. Nothing much else to pass on. They've found some other things in the flat pertaining to the book and I asked them to send that through to you. You can build up the mythology behind it all.'

'Will do,' said Patterson. 'I'll get on the way over to Gairlochy though, to look up the address. It's not that big a place—should be able to find her easily.'

'I'm going to join you. I might be a little behind you, but I'll get away now and see how long I take.'

'Do you want me to go straight there, or do you want me to do a bit of work first to build up this mythology?'

'You build the mythology up first. Take an hour and then get over.'

'You think she's in any danger?'

'Don't think so,' said Clarissa. 'What's the likelihood of her knowing anything? I mean, it would be in the book if you put the names down. She's an editor for the book.'

'Maybe they cut things from the book. So maybe she knows more.'

'In which case, she'll be being watched as well. She'll probably be dead by now,' said Clarissa. 'Get yourself over and find out what's going on. I'll be as quick as I can.'

'Should I take backup with me?'

'Don't wait for it. See if you can find someone to go with you from Glasgow, but to be honest, it's well out of the way for the Edinburgh police. We are going all the way over to Gairlochy. See if the local police can get there.'

'Okay, I'll speak to you when I've got something,' said Patterson.

The call closed, and Clarissa took a breath. She finished her coffee and went back to her car. She wasn't looking forward to the drive, but she'd best get started.Patterson had spent a couple of hours digging through the mythology. He was becoming more and more convinced that the people chasing down this gem were nutters. He was used to things making sense. The arts world seemed to be off its rocker. In saying that, he thought people who paid that much money for a painting were off their rocker, anyway.

* * *

He understood diamonds when you put them on the tips of drills. They were useful. He wasn't a man who sat and looked at things. That wasn't his way. Not to simply appreciate them. But he guessed he'd have to understand it. He'd have to embrace it. After all, he was working in the Arts team. Clarissa would soon teach him, soon demand his opinions on things.

She was funny, though. A real old Rottweiler. That's what they called her. Someone who could bare her teeth. Someone who didn't always play it clean. And yes, she had an incredible fondness for art. Every time he'd seen her talk about paintings or sculptures, any type of artwork at all, she was enthused, bubbling over it. Her way was something he found, frankly, difficult to embrace.

Patterson felt he saw money; he saw value. Clarissa saw beauty. Beauty wasn't a word that got associated with Clarissa easily. She was gutsy, rough. She was a bit of a brawler in some ways. And she didn't pull her punches. Refinement was not

85

Clarissa. And yet, she could talk evidentially about art. The history of art. What people saw in various items.

Pulling into Gairlochy, Patterson saw a village that was spread out. He'd been unsuccessful at organising the local police, who were thin on the ground compared to a city like Edinburgh. Pulling into a house, he simply asked where Lynn Green lived. He was pointed to four houses down, which meant a fair drive, and so continued along before parking up in a short driveway.

It was a cottage, and Patterson could see a car in the driveway. He stepped out just as the sun broke through the clouds and took a moment to embrace it. Yes, it had been tough yesterday, and it was still coming back to him. But he was still on his feet. He was still going. Probably okay, and he'd cope.

Looking up at the cottage, Patterson suddenly froze. The door was ajar. He strode up to it, ignoring the delightful flower bed, just off to the right, and climbed up the little step that led to the green door. Pushing the door back further, he heard it squeak. He then rapped it and shouted out, 'Police! This is the police. We're looking for Lynn Green. Can I come in?'

There was nothing. No answer. No movement within the house. It was incredibly still. Eric Patterson stepped in through the door, walked down the hallway, opening a door out to the lounge. There was no one there. He then took a walk round into the kitchen. No one. He came back into the hall, walked past the door to the living room and was about to take the stairs to where he presumed was a bedroom towards the front of the house. However, just after passing by the living room door, something hit him on the back of the head. Patterson blanked out.Clarissa had driven as hard as she could. She was worried. Had Patterson gone there? Was Patterson going to be okay?

* * *

He hadn't called when he'd arrived. He hadn't called to say he'd been talking to Lynn Green. The longer it went on before she arrived, Clarissa grew more disturbed. She called Macleod briefly, asking if he had heard from Patterson. But he said he had been out with Sabine, to talk to some lords. He had more to do. So, she'd closed down the call and continued her drive. She phoned Patterson, but he didn't pick up. As she got closer to the property, she felt more and more anxious.

Entering Gairlochy, Clarissa saw a lot of police cars around one cottage towards the far end of the village. She drove over quickly, stepping out and marching over, only to find a policeman coming towards her, waving his hands.

'No, no, no. We don't do any press here. I'm afraid you'll have to stay back. You'll have to—'

Clarissa reached inside her shawl and pulled out her warrant card.

'Sorry, Detective Inspector. By all means, come through, but what are you—what are you here for?' asked the constable.

'One of my DC's came up here, Eric Patterson. He spoken to any of you?'

'No. We're here because a walker called in a disturbance. They said police were in attendance, but we had dispatched no one.'

'What do you mean?' asked Clarissa. 'There were police in attendance.'

'We don't believe any of our people were in attendance. There may have been people impersonating us, however.'

Clarissa suddenly shook. Patterson was gone. Why? She ran forward into the cottage and started tearing around it. But of course, the police had already been through it, and there was nothing to find. She came back out and stood outside the cottage, shaking like a leaf.

'Are you all right?' asked a constable.

'Am I all right?' said Clarissa. 'No, I bloody well am not. Our man's missing. Lynn Green's missing. Her car's there. I assume that's her car.'

'It is,' said the sergeant.

Clarissa walked away from the house. She shouldn't have let him come on his own. She'd told him to get back up. She'd told him to—

She grabbed her mobile phone and dialled in a number and waited for Macleod to pick up.

'Yes, Macleod. What's up?'

'Patterson's missing,' said Clarissa.

'What do you mean, missing?'

'Came to interview a suspect. Hasn't talked to me since and he's not here. He's—'

'Why was he there on his own?' asked Macleod.

'I told him not to. I told him to take backup with him. I told him—'

'He should have waited for you. You're the one who told me he was vulnerable. You're the one worried about whether he's okay. I'm not happy about this, Clarissa. I'm not happy.'

Clarissa felt like she was being crushed. Everything she'd ever done so far was being stripped away because of this mistake, because of this error.

'We need to get on to it,' said Clarissa. 'Can you—'

'No, I can't,' said Macleod. 'You'll have to do it. you've got a police force with you there at the moment. Use them, go find Eric, and find him quick, and find me Lynn Green as well. I'm about to talk with Lord Harwich, so I haven't got time to do other things at the moment. I'll talk to you when I come out. But find him—make sure you find him,' said Macleod. 'Never should have been there on his own anyway,'

'I was half a country away,' said Clarissa, but she knew he was right. She was the boss, she should have told him, made it clear. There were two killers about, and now he was missing. More than that, Lynn Green was missing too,

Clarissa looked around the cottage, then looked at the surrounding countryside. She realised Patterson could be anywhere. Did anybody else know the manuscript? Was that why Lynn Green was missing? Had she been taken or just absconded? Would she be killed? Clarissa needed to get on the trail again.

Clarissa got inside her hire car for a moment, her mind still racing. *Somebody had dressed up as the police. They'd been caught out. They'd been—what had happened? What had happened with Patterson? He was gone now.*

In all the times, and all the trauma, she'd spent with him, she'd never let him go. She'd been there, she'd saved him. And she'd brought him back to this. Clarissa had been the one keen to see him get better. She'd been the one keen to make amends. Well, her amends had ended up a mess. Her best efforts could end up with him losing his life. Deep down, Clarissa was shaking. She wasn't sure what she was going to do next. But whatever it was going to be, she'd need to do it quick.

Chapter 11

Macleod closed down the call he had received from Clarissa and he was steaming inside. She'd wanted this. She wanted to keep it on an arts team basis. Macleod had his reservations, but he wanted to give her a chance, wanted to let her run with it, to show everybody what she could do. Instead, he now had someone missing or Patterson was missing, presumed kidnapped. Possibly the same people who blew off the head of Reginald McLean and dispatched Sheila Alcock.

He stood for a moment in the waiting room, where he'd been placed by a butler. Sabine Ferguson was with him, but had ignored him taking the call, instead perusing the artwork in the surrounding room. Macleod lifted his head and called her over quietly.

'Bad news, Patterson's gone missing. They found a link to the editor of Reginald McLean's book. That editor, Lynn Green, wasn't in her house when Patterson got there, or possibly was. Clarissa arrived later, after Patterson had gone in solo, and he—he's not there, and neither's Lynn Green.'

'Doesn't mean they're dead,' said Ferguson. 'We don't have to assume—'

'Thank you,' said Macleod. 'I realise that. But I realise they could also be in serious trouble if not dead already.'

'Do you want to organise anything? Do you want me to cover this lord business?'

'No,' said Macleod. 'I'm coming in with you on this one. See what this guy knows. Because somebody knows something. This isn't my first rodeo with rich people who think they can buy stuff,' said Macleod. 'People who think they own the world.'

'Okay,' said Sabine, 'but maybe not the best attitude to go in with.'

'And what sort of attitude would you want me to go in with? I've got someone down.'

'Maybe an attitude of let's work out what we can get out of this person. I know I haven't worked with you before, but these people—if you come in steaming, they'll run rings round you. We need to be a bit more subtle.'

Macleod looked away from Ferguson for a moment and then turned back. 'You're absolutely correct,' he said. 'This stuff around you.'

'The artwork, the statues and that.'

'These old collectibles.'

'You make it sound like it's a Panini sticker album,' said Ferguson. 'Aye, it's all good stuff. It's not unheard-of stuff either. Mostly stuff you'd be waving around and going, "Look what I've got." It's solid. Most of the painters are well known, if not completely famous. He's not hiding a Mona Lisa in here, if that's what you're asking.'

'As I understand it, they wouldn't hide them in here, anyway. There would be—'

'It would be much more secure,' said Ferguson. 'Some of

these paintings, though, in fairness, rare, are not particularly in demand. It's quite an ostentatious show, if I'm honest with you.'

'He's kept me waiting fifteen minutes. Do you realise that?'

'I'm very aware,' said Sabine, 'and to be honest, as a detective sergeant, that's quite normal. I thought he might have upped his game a bit for you though, Detective Chief Inspector. Make sure you say that. I'll make sure I'll call you that, too.'

The door behind them opened and an older man, dressed up in a smart suit, entered with a wave of his hand. Beside him was a man that everything in Macleod screamed security about.

He was chunky, had a face that looked like a bulldog, and one that wasn't taking any prisoners today. He was also snarling, mostly at Macleod. The man didn't walk, but moved one foot, then swung his entire body to put the next foot round in front of it and then followed with the first foot again. He was a brute, but Macleod was never scared by brutes. He had people on his team who can handle brutes. Ferguson looked like she would know what she was doing with a brute.

'Please forgive me for keeping you two back,' said the man. 'My name is Lord Harwich. I'm sure you've heard of me.'

Macleod shook his head in the negative deliberately.

'Well, maybe someone more senior would know.'

'My name's Detective Chief Inspector Macleod and I kind of hope you've maybe heard of me. Most people are pretty prompt when I come to call.'

'Oh,' said the man, and turned and put his hand out to Sabine. 'You must be his good lady.'

'I'm Detective Sergeant Sabine Ferguson. The Detective Chief Inspector is the one fronting this investigation.'

'Investigation?' queried Lord Harwich. 'What are you investigating, my good man?'

If he 'good mans' me again,' thought Macleod, *'I'll punch him in his teeth.'*

Macleod really didn't have time for people with money. He had come from Lewis. And he hadn't had a lot of money when he was growing up. Most of the people were decent. Most people were. Those who thought themselves above—those who used their money to employ people at ridiculously low rates—would always receive Macleod's ire.

'I'm investigating a jewel you may have heard of. The Esoteric *T-ear.'*

'The Esoteric *T-air,'* countered Lord Harwich. 'Indeed, of course, I've heard of it.'

He has, hasn't he, thought Macleod. *He knew it wasn't T-ear but T-air.* 'Can I ask you something? Have you ever sought it?' asked Macleod.

'Sought it as in to acquire it?' asked Lord Harwich. 'I absolutely have. Quite an interesting piece.'

'Really? I thought it would have been below your standing,' said Macleod. 'I was told it cost little.'

'Be very careful with valuations,' said Lord Harwich. 'A man of the streets like yourself would be unaware. I'm sure your sergeant here is more aware. She seems to have a keen eye. I see that you've cast a glance over some of the more important parts of my collection.'

'The Detective Chief Inspector was asking about the Esoteric Tear,' said Sabine.

'Of course he was,' said Lord Harwich. 'As I told you, the price tag says it is of little value. In itself, the diamond doesn't look great, but the history behind it is quite something if you know it.'

'Do you know it?' asked Macleod.

'Yes,' said Lord Harwich.

'Well, if you'd care to enlighten me.'

'It's an ancient piece. Very, very old. Or at least, that's the rumour. It's never been confirmed, its age. People haven't tested it. Acquired recently by the Scottish Museums. They were taking it on tour, I believe. I put an offer to them. Well, not directly, of course. Via some of my contacts. I was offering a couple of thousand for it. But they said no. No, they wouldn't sell, so I upped it to what its mythology would value it at.'

'How much?' asked Macleod.

'Well, one doesn't like to say.'

'One will say, or one will join me down at the station to say,' said Macleod.

'No need to get your knickers in a twist, Detective Chief Inspector. Let's say it was at least six figures I offered.'

'Worth that sort of money, is it?'

'A drop in the pan? A blip in the sky? No. It's not an unfamiliar sum to me, but one that would have been worth it.'

'Why?' asked Macleod. 'Why do you want something worth £2,000 so much that you're going to pay six figures for it?'

'Because of what it is. Some people think it's a portal. A portal to a better place when the end times come.'

'Is that the whole mythology?' asked Sabine.

'The gist of it. At least what was in the books back in the day. They were written in Sanskrit, so sometimes translation's not that good, as it gets passed down through the centuries. Books get re-transcribed, get re-written. But the guts of it stays. Quite a relic, as opposed to a gem.'

'Only a relic if it actually does what it says.'

'Oh, come, come, Detective Chief Inspector,' said Lord Harwich. 'Plenty of people believe in it. Whether or not it does it is irrelevant. I'd be the one owning it. I'd be the one that people would have to bow to, to come and see it. Certain people would not enjoy that. It'd be worth the six figures.'

'Can't you just pull up in a nice old Rolls Royce?' asked Macleod. 'Make them jealous like that.'

'I don't use the word Philistine often, Detective Chief Inspector.'

'And don't use it now,' said Macleod. 'Tell me, have you ever heard of a man called Aboud?'

'Yes?' Macleod swung himself round behind Lord Harwich and came up close to him. Lord Harwich didn't move, and neither did his protector who remained standing in the corner.

Macleod turned away again. 'And where do you know Aboud from?'

'Aboud tried to acquire the item for me.'

'From whom?' asked Macleod.

'Well, you probably wouldn't have heard of her. She's a go-between. A dealer.'

'Fence?' offered Macleod.

'Oh, let's not use the sullied terms. Let's talk properly, shall we? Sheila Alcock has never been a fence. Sheila understands the items she acquires. Sheila has taste, she has clarity, she understands what she is going to acquire for someone. Delights in being a part of history, delights in being a part of—'

'So, you didn't pay her then?' said Macleod. 'She just did it for this prestige you talk about?'

'She takes ten per cent like anyone,' said Lord Harwich. 'Prestige doesn't pay the bills, and she still has bills to pay.'

'Well, at least she'll no longer be worried about that.' Macleod spun round, his eyes fixed on Lord Harwich.

'Why?' the man asked.

'Sheila Alcock is dead. Throat slashed. Happened just before one of my officers got there.'

'Let's hope you're not as tardy if I'm under threat,' said Lord Harwich, without missing a beat. Macleod shot a glance at Sabine, who gave a shake of her head.

'Was Sheila looking for the Esoteric Tear for you?'

'She was the one who contacted the museum. She was the one who couldn't get it for me. The museum was not obliging.'

'It's now been stolen,' said Macleod. 'Did you organise that?'

'If I did, you think I would tell you?' said Lord Harwich. 'It's a rather redundant question.'

'A redundant question that you haven't answered,' said Macleod. 'I have two witnesses here, myself and Sabine.'

'And my man in the corner?'

'That painting over there would be a more reliable witness than your man in the corner,' said Macleod. 'Answer the question. Did you organise for it to be taken? To be stolen?'

'Absolutely not,' said Lord Harwich. 'How was it taken, anyway?'

'It was stolen from a trailer while on display to the public out by Urquhart Castle.' Macleod saw Harwich smile. 'What's funny?' asked Macleod.

'Urquhart Castle. You'd think it would be safe out there, wouldn't you? Your own sergeant, isn't it? Clarissa Urquhart. She likes her art.'

'Detective Inspector Urquhart,' said Macleod, 'was the one who recovered all the gems that were stolen along with it. But somebody was wise enough to take the one with the smallest value, at least monetary value.'

'What can I say,' said Lord Harwich, 'None of that was my doing. I'll admit I was seeking it, to have in the collection so I could lord it over a few other people.'

'Are you one of the Dwellers,' Macleod asked. 'Are you one of the people who would look to inhabit what the gem would produce for you at the end times?'

'Really, Inspector, are you the one to be taken away in the rapture? Would you talk about your mythology? Would you openly say you'll be there? One can never tell what the end times will be. But we all have our beliefs, don't we? If you'll excuse me,' said Lord Harwood suddenly, 'I've got to deal with a situation on the estate. Seems that I have a debtor in one house. If you need me, I am here. Do make sure you have an appointment.'

'If I need you again, I'll tell you where the station is and where to meet me,' said Macleod. 'Or have you been there before?'

Harwood smiled. 'It's been such a delight to finally meet Detective Chief Inspector Macleod. Seen you on the telly.'

Macleod turned and nodded to Sabine and the pair made their way back out from the waiting room to the car parked in the large driveway of the stately home. Once inside the car, Macleod let Ferguson take the wheel, and they drove off out through Grantown on Spey, where Macleod told her to pull over. They entered a small coffee shop, Macleod ordering, telling Sabine that this first one was on him. When the coffee arrived, he turned to the Northern Irish woman.

'Did you notice anything?'

'Yes,' she said. 'He did not frisk us once. With all those valuable items there, we weren't looked at. We didn't even get asked for ID.'

'No, we didn't,' said Macleod. 'I also went round the back of him. I took up a very dangerous position and his man didn't even react. Harwich knew about Sheila Alcock's death. He wasn't shocked when I told him. He knows what's going on here. What got me was his man wasn't even bothered. He doesn't know who I am. And he didn't check. And he didn't react when I went close. I think somebody's an instigator. I don't know how we're going to prove it.'

'Did you notice the other thing?' asked Sabine. 'I was a bit surprised, didn't think it would be something that would go down well. I thought a lot of these people had classier security than this.'

'He wasn't security. I don't know who that man was,' said Macleod, 'but he wasn't security. But what he had was this.' Macleod pulled a notebook from inside his jacket pocket and put it on the table. He began drawing a symbol.

'Let me do that for you, sir,' said Sabine.

Macleod raised his eyebrows, and she ripped off the paper, and crumpled it up. Then, on a blank piece, Sabine drew out a perfect representation of a tattoo Macleod had seen on the man's wrist.

'That will mean something,' said Macleod. 'We need to find out what. If somebody's displaying symbols, they may be society-based, maybe gang-related—who knows? We'll get this to Jona, get it to some of the other people within the team, see if we can dig up what that is.'

'Yes, sir,' said Sabine. 'Can I just ask one thing? Why did we order this coffee with cups to take away if we're going to sit here?'

'I can't draw in the car,' said Macleod. 'You thought that was bad on the table? Grab your cup. Patterson's missing. We need to get cracking.'

Chapter 12

Clarissa Urquhart sat on her hotel room bed, trying her best not to stare at the mirror directly opposite. Her eyes were red, having cried many tears that day. Pats was missing. Eric Patterson, the man who she'd protected, the man whose throat she'd covered with her hands as the blood ran thick over them, whose life she'd preserved against all the odds. Pats was missing, and in her head she couldn't get away from the fact he could be dead.

Lynn Green could be dead, too. Clarissa had been so excited, back in the Arts team, and now there were two bodies already. And there may be two more. She lifted her head up to look in the mirror.

'Come on, Clarissa,' she said to herself. 'Now's not the time to fall apart. It's the time to fight. The time to push through, become something.'

Macleod had been a positive bastion when he had called her earlier. He had questions about Lord Harwich, about his artwork, what he got involved with. He also had some leads. And being Macleod, he'd be dogged. He'd push through.

But he was taking most of the work over to Sabine. Of course, he didn't really know her. But he'd have to trust her.

After all, she was part of the team, and they were only just getting to know each other.

On a lighter note, Clarissa was also missing her little green sports car, for it was still stuck in Glasgow, waiting to be picked up. The hire car was sitting out in the car park, visible from her window, but she wasn't concerned about it. It wasn't interesting. It wasn't something she wanted to stare at. Her little green car always comforted her. Right now, she wanted to get in it, and drive . . . and not stop driving.

Clarissa stood up and walked over to the window, looking out at the hire car. It wasn't good. Everything was so cramped these days. They said it was modern. But it did everything for you. It took her half the time to switch everything off so she could drive properly. It kept telling her whenever she crossed the central reservation.

Crossing the central lines didn't mean she was out of control. She needed to steer back. No, she didn't. She crossed them deliberately. And she was drifting. Yes, but she was drifting for a reason. Evil, modern-day piece of junk!

It really wasn't on taking everything out on a poor little car. A car that was sitting doing nothing. A car that was quite irrelevant, really. She sighed and went to turn away, but then she stopped. *There's somebody out there*, she thought. *Someone in the trees.*

Her first instinct would have been to look, to stare through the window. But something inside her told her not to. She turned away and desperately looked around the room. She grabbed a hairbrush and walked back to the window. Before her reflection, she brushed her hair. But she wasn't. She was staring just beyond her car.

There was somebody there, she was sure of it. At the

moment they were trying to stay still, but when she was looking earlier, they'd moved. They'd turned slightly, so their profile was on show. Clarissa kept brushing her hair, kept watching to see if there was anyone else there. Slowly, she turned and put her brush down.

Clarissa walked out to the car, trying not to appear as if she was searching, but she let her eyes dart around the scene. She opened the car, pretending to take something from the glove box, locked it, and made her way back inside.

Soon she passed by her own window again. There it was. It was a shadow, a figure, watching. Clarissa turned away and boiled the kettle in her room, taking a cup over. She then lifted out her pyjamas, making sure they could be seen through the window before she closed the blinds over.

As soon as she'd done so, she left her own room; the door closed behind her. Instead of heading for the main entrance—which would allow her to walk round to her car as she'd done a few minutes before—she headed off for the emergency exit at the other end of the hotel.

It wasn't a large hotel, but the exit was out of sight. This allowed her to walk out of the rear door and stop, peering from the corner of the building towards her car. They were still there. They were definitely still there.

Slowly, she crept over into the trees at the rear of the car park. She froze behind one of them as a car entered the car park, its lights briefly whizzing past her own location. Clarissa was tight up against the tree, thinking that she couldn't be seen. She hoped not. She still had her tartan trews on and a blouse that was salmon pink. It wasn't the best for creeping around in, but it would have to do.

Slowly, she crept along the rear of the car park through the trees until she was within fifteen feet of the man who was watching her room. There was nobody else with him, nobody else near. Carefully, Clarissa crept along again, getting up behind the man.

She'd have to jump him quickly. She'd have to surprise him, take him down directly from behind. Clarissa threw an arm around his neck, reaching out for one of his arms to drive it up behind his back. The man grunted, falling down to his knees. Clarissa tried to follow up on him, but he was savvy. He fell forward, sending her toppling over the front of him.

Clarissa scrambled up to her feet to see the man rise. He reached forward with both hands and she lashed out, kicking him in the knee. The man grunted, but a hand had her blouse and pulled her towards him. He hit her on the side, but Clarissa reached round and clawed across his face. Her nails scratched into him and again, he yelped.

Her hands fought for purchase on him, one finding his neck. It wasn't a correct police hold. It wasn't the way you apprehended people, but at the moment Clarissa was a woman on her own and desperate. She should have hit him in the back of the head to begin with, knocked him out, but now she forced her thumb up and into his Adam's apple, constricting his neck.

She heard him choke. He reached out with his own hands, grabbing her shoulder roughly. She ignored the pain, driving home her advantage. He coughed and struggled. She was going to win.

Something hit her across the back of the head, and she tumbled forward. She wasn't knocked out cold, but the blow was strong. Instead, as she fell, she turned her shoulder and rolled onto her back. Looking up, she saw two figures now.

One, the man who she'd been wrestling with.

But there was another shorter figure whose face was too dark to see. Their body was androgynous. It could have been a man or a woman. They turned and ran. Clarissa thought about standing up and chasing after them, but she stopped. If she ran after them and caught up with them, what was she going to do? They'd just—well, they could do whatever they wanted, for there were two of them. She was outmanned.

Instead, groggily holding the back of her head, she stumbled across the car park, making for then entrance to the hotel. Stumbling inside, she made her way over to the reception desk. She stood for a moment, panting, and could see a man's hands on the desk in front of her. *Good*, she thought. *There's somebody here. Someone I can talk to.*

'I'm Detective Inspector Clarissa Urquhart, staying in room 23,' she said. 'I've just been attacked. A couple of men out the back have been watching my room. Watching from behind my car. I think it's two men. It was certainly one man. Maybe a woman. Hard to tell. Strange figure. But I need you to phone the police. We need to get some people here. Do you understand me?'

'Yes,' a voice said quickly.

'Can you do that for me? Can you phone the police? You'll need to give them a description. He's got black hair. I think he was five foot eight. The other one maybe five six. Didn't see the hair on the other one but it was long. First one was a stocky build, and he had jeans on, not sure about much else. Please, you need to get the police for me.'

'Why do you need the police?' asked the person.

Clarissa was bent over, wheezing at the desk. The fight had taken more out of her than she had realised. *Is this some sort of idiot? Why do I need the police? I've just been involved in a scuffle. I'm an officer. I'm looking for help.'*

'Don't question me. I need you to phone the police. The local police. How long do they take to get police up here? It's not safe at the moment, okay? Can you get the police for me, please? Can you get the police? I need the police.'

'Why?' asked the voice.

'Because it's not safe. Get the police.'

'The police are already here,' said the voice.

The accent had changed. Was she imagining this? That sounded like a voice she knew. Slowly, Clarissa lifted her head. She followed the hands up to the arms and half recognised the suit that was being worn. She looked higher and Patterson was smiling back at her.

'Police are already here,' he said. 'Don't see why we need any more.'

'Seriously,' she said, 'you've let me blow a gasket here, sit in that room, and cry my eyes out.'

Patterson came round from behind the desk and took Clarissa by the arm. 'You'd best get back to your room. I take it the curtains are drawn. I don't really want to be seen here.'

'Where's the desk person? Have they seen you?'

'No. I put a call in for them. They're off attending to a room. The good people in that room won't know anything about why they've called them.'

'That's very savvy of you,' said Clarissa. And she stopped and hit him. 'What the hell were you doing? Running off alone. What were you doing?'

'Let's not have a domestic here,' said Patterson. 'I don't care if you're the boss, you're not allowed to punch me.'

'Punch you? I'll bloody kill you!' said Clarissa under her breath.

She led him down the corridor, used her keycard on the reader, and opened the door. Patterson helped her in and laid her down on the bed before collecting one of her towels, soaking it and bringing it over to use as a compress on the back of her head.

'You bloody idiot,' she said. 'Macleod's raging. Raging at me as well. He's—'

'Well, he's going to be happy I'm here.'

'Are you all right?'

'I'm fine,' said Patterson. 'Just a bump on my head. Somebody was there when I arrived. Somebody worried and very, very frightened. Give me a moment.'

'No,' said Clarissa. 'Before you go, come here.'

Patterson walked round the bed towards her. She threw her arms forward, grabbed him and pulled him in tight, holding on to him. 'Don't you bloody well scare me like that. We got you, though. You're all right. Bloody hell. I'm so glad you're all right.'

'Easy. Look, I've got to get someone.'

'Do you need any help?' said Clarissa.

'Just give me your key card. I'll be back in a minute.'

She watched Patterson walk out and then collapsed onto her bed. The compress on the back of her head was helping, but not a lot. Soon she heard the door open again.

Clarissa was twitchy, even though she knew Patterson was coming back. She smiled as he walked through, but he quickly pushed someone in front of her.

'Not only am I okay,' he said, 'but there's someone you need to meet. This is Lynn Green. She was the editor for Reginald

McLean's book, and she's a little scared at the moment. Lynn, this is my boss, Detective Inspector Clarissa Urquhart. She's not feeling too good at the moment, and apparently, it's all my fault.'

Chapter 13

'Okay,' said Clarissa, 'I'm delighted you're here. I'm delighted you're both here, but what on earth happened?'

'Well, this is the thing,' said Patterson. 'The door was open when I arrived at Lynn's house, so I made my way in. I was sneaking around quietly when somebody clopped me on the back of the head.'

'That was me,' said Lynn. 'Sorry, but I didn't know who you were. We'd had police officers turn up earlier, but they weren't our local police officers. I'd heard on the news what had happened to Reg, and I was wary, to say the least. So, I didn't answer the door to them, and I hid. But they opened the front door. I didn't come out though after that to close it, in case they were watching.'

'Probably saved your life,' said Patterson. 'I went in and got attacked. Lynn hid away, and I got myself back out.'

'I was worried about the house and what was going on. In the meantime, I'd run off,' said Lynn. 'There's a small bridge not far down from where I am. I hid underneath it. I was five hours under there.'

'So how did the two of you get together?' asked Clarissa.

'I'm a little confused.'

'I went back into the house,' said Patterson. 'So, Lynn had come out of the house after attacking me. I was out cold but when I recovered, there were sirens, police sirens. I almost ran out to them to say it was me in there, but I thought better of it.'

'Good job you did,' said Lynn. 'They weren't our actual police officers.'

'They weren't even real police cars, Clarissa,' said Patterson. 'They weren't decorated at all; it was just a siren. Cleverly done, though. So, I hid out. They came in and searched the place completely, and then waited outside to see what else was going to happen.'

'I searched the area rather than just hide,' said Patterson. 'I snuck out the back and eventually came to the bridge and found Lynn hiding underneath it. Thought best that we stay there for a moment. I saw them before I left the house asking a nearby hitchhiker about who was inside.'

'The hitchhiker eventually phoned the police, thinking they'd seen somebody else,' said Clarissa, 'and then the real police turned up. So, when I was there, they had searched the house and nobody was about.'

'At that point, we legged it,' said Patterson. 'It took me a while to convince Lynn, but she came with me, and we hid out watching the house. When you turned up, I could see the car, but I couldn't get near you. Then I traced you back to this hotel.'

'How'd you do that?' asked Clarissa.

'It's not difficult, is it? Not that many hotels around here, and you would not go far. I'd disappeared from that house. I reckoned you would have made a search pattern to look for me. Although, Macleod probably told you not to. Probably told you to follow the evidence.'

'Speaking of which, we should really contact him.'

'Well, what's our next move?' asked Patterson.

'The two people watching this hotel, clearly they must have thought someone's going to come and contact me, because they know they haven't got you. You've disappeared. They've seen you in the building, Pats. They don't know where Lynn is, so they're coming to me to find Lynn. We need to get Lynn far away from here and to somewhere safe.'

'Can Macleod do that?'

'Sure, he's got the power to pull safe houses. He'll find something from somewhere. The key thing is that nobody else knows that. I'm sorry, Lynn,' said Clarissa, 'but I think your life's in danger. I think you might know something they don't want others to know.'

'I know nothing. He's already asked me if I know any other names?'

'Really,' said Clarissa, 'you truly don't know any of the names? At no point did Reg mention them to you? Did Reg have them in an earlier draft that you had seen? Because if there's nothing in the book that gives anyone away, why would you be a target? I'm a bit confused,' said Clarissa. 'I understand if you're not willing to talk to us at the moment, because let's face it, you've had a heck of a time so far. But I am who I say I am. You can check the ID. It's in that jacket over there.'

Lynn looked across at Clarissa. 'I told you I don't know any names.'

Clarissa swung her legs off the bed and winced as she walked across, took out her ID and showed her warrant card to Lynn,

'This could be fake,' said Lynn.

'Can I have a word, Patterson,' said Clarissa,

Together, the two of them walked to the door of the hotel room. 'She's scared, Pats,' said Clarissa.

'I know. It took everything I had to get her just to come with me.'

'How's she going to know we're the real police?' asked Clarissa.

'Well, she's not trusting warrant cards so other than actually driving into Inverness station and saying, "Look it's us", I don't know. Is she going to come that far with us? We can only get there in a car.'

'We don't want to get there in a car. At the moment, my car's in Glasgow. I could stick the two of you in the boot and we could drive up through the night to pick mine up from the station in Glasgow. She'll know then who we are.'

'Why don't you leave?' said Patterson. 'Drive up to the station, pick your car up. I'll meet you somewhere near here. You'll know then if they are still on you. I mean, if they're tailing you out of Glasgow, you'll spot them.'

'Good idea. What are you going to do?'

'Stay in here. No one's seen us come into this room. They're going to see you going out of it. Once you've headed off, we'll make our own way. Bring the map up on the phone, please.'

Clarissa did as asked and showed it to Patterson.

'We'll meet you there, that roadside. Okay? Pull by, stop, thirty seconds. If we don't get in, go. Something's happened and I've gone elsewhere. But I'll phone you if that's the case, or maybe just text you.'

'Okay, do you want to tell Lynn what we're doing? I think it might come better from you.'

Clarissa let Patterson explain what was about to happen.

Lynn gave a nod, but she didn't seem entirely happy. Patterson said she could run for it whenever they went out into the countryside. It wouldn't be a problem.

Clarissa fixed her hair with a brush in front of the mirror and tried to sort out her red eyes before packing up her stuff. Putting it into a case, she left it in the wardrobe.

'I'll phone them to send it up to me later on.'

'That's a good idea. Tell you what,' said Patterson; 'don't phone Macleod until you're well on the way.'

'Of course not,' said Clarissa. 'But be there, okay? It's going to take me the best part of, oh, a couple of hours up to Glasgow and back out again. I'll see you at three in the morning.'

'Don't be late,' said Patterson. 'I'm on edge as it is.'

Clarissa gave him a hug and then left the room. She strode out to her car, climbed in, and drove off. She was soon aware that somebody was following her, but she was quite happy with this. Clarissa didn't pull any stunts, and just kept driving.

The car tailed her all the way out onto the major roads and back to Glasgow. At the Glasgow station, she dropped her car in the car park, advising the desk sergeant that someone would come from the hire firm to pick it up. He handed her the keys to her own car.

'That's a neat little thing.'

'Has anybody been in it?' she asked.

'I told them who owned it. I don't think anybody dares.'

'Good,' said Clarissa. 'That's what I like to hear.' She jumped into the green car and drove off initially, heading further into Glasgow, stopping by a hotel. She made her way inside and then sat and watched out the window. After an hour, the tail that had followed her disappeared. She jumped back in the car and headed back towards Spean Bridge. She had to drive at speed because she was now behind time. But at three o'clock in the morning, she pulled up quickly in front of a little gate leading into a farmer's field.

After fifteen seconds, she was sweating. *Where are they?* she thought. At twenty-five seconds she heard the gate rattle, Patterson in a horse whisper urging, 'Go, go, go.' And the next minute he was sitting beside her in the passenger seat, Lynn hiding with her head down low in the back.

'Are we off?'

'Yes,' said Clarissa. 'We're off.'

As she drove through the dark, Clarissa used the hands-free function on her phone and placed a call to Macleod.

'What?' It wasn't a typical Macleod response. He was clearly worried.

'I've got him,' said Clarissa. 'I've got him, and we need to go somewhere, because I've also got Lynn Green, the editor of Reginald McLean's book. She doesn't trust us because she's had fake police come to the house. I think when she meets you, she'll trust us. After all, everybody knows you. Got to show her the celebrity before she'll come on board.'

'You really think her life's at risk?' asked Macleod.

'What do you think? Reginald McLean's dead. Sheila Alcock's dead, too. Don't take any risks on this one, Seoras. Give me a safe house. Text me the address.'

'No,' said Macleod. 'Meet me. Meet me at—Boat of Garten.'

'I'm in my green car,' said Clarissa.

'Exactly,' said Macleod. 'I'll be in a car nobody knows. And we'll take Lynn to the safe house. And then I'll bring you back to your car.'

'You want me to leave it in the Boat of Garten in the middle of the morning? Anybody could have a go at it.'

'Her life's at risk. We do this carefully. How's Patterson?'

'Bump on the head, Lynn hit him. I'm okay, too. I got hit.'

'Well, get up the road. I'll meet you there. I'll sort out this safe house for us.'

'Oh, Seoras,' said Clarissa. 'I thought it was easier on the Arts team. I thought things were meant to be quieter.'

'It was never the murder team that was the problem,' said Macleod. 'It's you. You're the one causing all this trouble.'

She stopped for a moment and thought about it, and then she laughed. 'You had me there,' she said. 'You had me.'

'It is three in the morning,' said Macleod. 'It wasn't difficult. See you shortly.'

'Where are we going now?' asked Patterson.

'We're going to Boat of Garten.' And then she leaned over, quickly shouting into the rear of the car. 'Lynn, you'll be pleased to hear I'm going to take you to meet a celebrity.'

'Who?' she asked.

'One of the most famous policemen in the Highlands.'

'I'm not going to see him.'

'You are indeed. I'm going to introduce you to Detective Chief Inspector Seoras Macleod. I'm sure you'll recognise him from the telly.'

She nodded. 'Okay. Where are we going?'

'I don't know. We're meeting him in Boat of Garten. After that, he's taking you somewhere safe. We're taking this very seriously,' said Clarissa. 'And you'll be staying there until we know it's over.'

Lynn nodded. 'Okay,' she said. 'I'll trust you when I see him.'

Clarissa drove through the night, but soon heard Lynn snoring from the back seat. Clearly, she was trusting them more already. Patterson sat beside Clarissa, but he almost seemed relaxed now.

'You're never like this in my car,' she said.

'No. It's nighttime. There's not so many cars to hit.'

She punched him on the arm.

'I said you can't do that.'

'Soak it up, sunshine. Any more wisecracks like that and there'll be plenty more.'

'Well, at least you're glad I'm okay. Even if you're going to kill me yourself.'

She could have so punched him again. 'You had me worried,' she said. 'You had me really worried.'

Chapter 14

Clarissa sat in the back of the car as it pulled up at a small residential house in Culloden. They were just to the east of Inverness, and the car, with its tinted windows, didn't seem to draw any attention.

'It's a normal sort of house,' said Macleod. 'The kind you find on every estate, but we fill it occasionally. With holiday makers, apparently.'

'I didn't know we had these,' said Clarissa. 'I take it you borrowed it from a friend?'

'No,' said Macleod. 'But the less we talk about that, the better. Let's get inside. Anyway, I believe there should be enough groceries to keep us going for a day or two. At least, that's what the landlord said.'

'Landlord?' queried Clarissa.

'These things are always stocked up for three days at least.'

Macleod clambered out of the front passenger seat, while Clarissa removed herself from the rear. She spun round the other side of the car, opened the rear door, and led Lynn Green over to where Macleod was opening the front door of the house. Patterson, who had driven, followed them in after locking the car. Closing the door behind them, Macleod made sure the blinds in the living room were closed over.

'We need to be discreet when we're here,' said Macleod, 'don't let any of the neighbours look in. When you're upstairs, especially at night, get the curtains closed early.'

'Will we have anybody watching out for us, protecting?' asked Clarissa.

'No,' said Macleod. 'Don't tell anyone at the station where we are either. They don't know. The only people that know where this is, is you, me, Patterson here, Lynn and, well, one other person. But I'll not tell you who that is.'

'I won't ask then,' said Clarissa. 'Shall I put the kettle on?'

'That'll be good,' said Patterson. 'That was a reasonable drive up and I'm feeling pretty parched. See if there are any sandwiches, too.'

'You'd almost think I wasn't the boss the way you said that.'

Patterson shot a look at Clarissa. 'I worked for my lunch,' he said. 'I drove all the way up here,'

Clarissa saw Macleod standing behind Patterson, smiling, as Patterson left the room to use the facilities. Macleod strode up close to Clarissa.

'He's certainly becoming more like himself, isn't he? Or at least what I think he was like before all this started.'

'I said he needed to get back out. But he's just seen a man have his head blown apart.'

'I said he's looking better,' said Macleod. 'I didn't say he was over it. Or he was fine.'

'Oh, cheer up,' said Clarissa. 'We're all getting it in the neck at the moment. Anyway, what are we doing now?'

'Well, you get the drinks sorted, then we'll sit down and have a bit of a round table. Oh, I've got somebody else still to arrive.'

'Have you told her where this is, then?'

'No,' said Macleod. 'I'm just about to. I wanted to make sure we were safely installed before Ferguson knew.'

'Why? Are you wary of her? You unsure if she's going to—'

'No,' said Macleod. 'It's just that nobody else knew you were coming up here except me. Excuse me a minute.'

Clarissa heard an awkward conversation with Macleod on the phone. When he came back through, she had put coffees on a small table in the dining room. Lynn Green was now sitting at the table with Patterson. Soon, the four of them were crowded round, drinking the hot liquid.

'So, what do we do now, boss?' asked Clarissa.

'One, you're the boss regarding running this show. And two, we're still waiting for someone,' replied Macleod.

There came a knock at the door. A few moments later, Macleod walked to it before bringing Sabine Ferguson into the room. Lynn Green looked up suspiciously.

'Detective Sergeant Sabine Ferguson from Glasgow. She's part of the team,' said Macleod. 'We can't leave it with just Patterson being a lively one amongst us.'

'Cheek,' said Clarissa. Sabine sat down, noticed there wasn't a drink for her, and made her way to the kitchen before coming back with a glass of milk.

'Right then,' said Macleod. 'I'm not happy. We've got two deaths on our hands, one by a professional hitman. I think we need to call in a lot more people. I think we need to make this a bigger investigation, possibly even go and talk to the special services, the ones that do things in the quiet.'

'No,' said Clarissa, indignantly. 'No way. We should play it quiet. Much quieter. Much, much quieter.'

'Why?' spat Macleod.

'You get the Secret Service involved in this, those idiots, and they won't understand the subtleties of the art world. I know the people I'm dealing with here. And if they smell a rat, they'll get out of it. They'll go. We'll never see that diamond again. And they'll still cause trouble. They won't stop going after it. All it'll do is get us off the trail. At the moment, we're on the trail. We should stay on it.'

'It's not much of a trail, though, is it?' said Patterson.

Clarissa glared at him. 'We still have Ali Ralston to talk to.'

'Well, that's right,' said Ferguson. 'She might generate something, but beyond that, what else have we got?'

'Well, I'll keep up with the teams that are investigating the murders,' said Macleod. 'I'll keep the forces separate, though, reporting in to me. They may dig out something but they may want their own murder teams to go after it.'

'They can do what they want,' said Clarissa, 'as long as they keep out of the way. Can't spook people.'

'No, but if there's been murders and nobody's investigating, it's going to look pretty suspicious,' said Macleod. 'I'll get them to run everything through me first. Make sure I understand what's happening. Give the green light to things. That satisfy you?'

'Okay,' said Clarissa.

'Anyway,' said Macleod, 'the diamond's probably out of the country by now.'

'No, it's not,' said Clarissa. 'The people that are after this are zealots. It's a cult in some ways. They won't want the diamond out of the country, I reckon.'

'You're right there,' said Lynn. 'From everything that Reginald said, when we were discussing the book, these people are fanatics. Nutters, I suppose, although he would never use that word. Reg thought that the Esoteric Tear was a possibility.'

'He actually believed the hype around it?' asked Macleod.

'No, he thought it was a possibility. He certainly didn't become a genuine believer. He had a deep interest in it, but he wasn't one hundred percent convinced. That's why I took the job. I wanted to be the editor of a reasonable book, not one by a nutter. Doesn't look good on the CV,' said Lynn. 'If you produce something that's reasonable, well, it'll get you more work. The other thing is, of course, the book then got stopped by them. Reg got the squeeze put on him. That's why it's hard to find.'

'So,' said Macleod, 'I'll control the other teams that are investigating the murders. What are you going to do?'

'Ferguson, Patterson, and myself, we'll do what we're good at. We'll trace the diamond. And, yes, we'll start with Ali Ralston. There are other avenues I can go down, too.'

'Well, stay safe with them. Make sure you back each other up this time. And Patterson,' said Macleod, 'no charging in alone, even though it looks safe.'

Patterson went to argue, but Clarissa shook her head, showing he should just shut up and take his medicine.

'Well, it looks like we're off to see Ali Ralston then,' said Clarissa.

'Not yet,' said Macleod. He pulled out his notebook and threw down the sketch of the bodyguard's tattoo that Sabine Ferguson had drawn.

'I haven't had any luck looking for that. It's not coming up in any databases,' said Sabine.

'It's in the book,' said Lynn Green.

'Are you sure?' asked Macleod.

'Absolutely. I've seen that. It's in the book. Look, it's in the manuscript. Hang on. It's stored away in my files. I'll just dig it up.'

The woman pulled her phone out of her pocket and went to use it. But Clarissa took it off her. She held the on-off button hard until the phone had closed itself down. Then she put it on the sideboard.

'You don't use that here. Of all the people they can hack into or look at, it'll be you. We're the police force and will be on the move. We won't necessarily be here. Although we'll try to keep someone with you at all times.'

'But it's just the manuscript. I've just got to go into my—'

'Tell me your details. Tell me how to get in. And I'll get someone elsewhere to do it.'

Clarissa wrote the details down and then placed a call from the landline of the house to the Inverness Police Station. The other end was picked up.

'This is DC Ross. How can I help you?'

'Als, I need you to do some snooping on somebody's account for me. Get in and pull some files.'

'I don't work for you anymore. In fact, I'm nearly the same rank as you.'

'You moved up, I moved up, Als. Don't worry about it. But, if I need to run it past Hope, by all means, but you need to do this. Look, here are the details.'

Clarissa rhymed off what she wanted Ross to do, including the access details provided by Lynn Green.

'Tell Hope the big boss says it's okay to use you.'

'He's there with you, is he?'

'Oh yeah, he's here with me. Wondering why you haven't got it done already, Als.' Macleod started to laugh.

'I'll find it then,' said Ross. 'So, it's a book manuscript I'm wanting. Okay, give me fifteen minutes.'

Clarissa put the phone away, and they sat back down again.

'Any more ideas?' asked Macleod.

'Not really,' she said. 'Tell you what, why don't we get another round of coffee in? See if we can get it ready before Als calls back. Bet you he won't make it in time.'

'Of course he will,' said Macleod. Macleod sat, clearly waiting for Clarissa to move. In the end, Sabine Ferguson got up and grabbed the cups. When she came back, she placed them down in front of everyone.'

'I've no idea if you take milk, sugar, water, or you like coffee or tea. It's what it is. Drink it up at your leisure.'

Macleod was smiling.

'What's up with you, Seoras?'

'Thirty seconds before you walked back in, Ross called. He's just firing over the manuscript now.'

Soon, a PDF was opened up on Clarissa's laptop. It didn't take long to spot the tattoo image.

'Yeah, there it is. He's a member of the Dwellers,' said Lynn 'A rank known as deacon. To be honest, Reg didn't really know all the exact ranks because they were in Sanskrit. He sort of made them up and attributed them similar to church names. But it's quite high up. I mean he's one of the operators within the group. He's not just an acolyte or a follower.'

'He was beside Lord Harwich,' said Macleod. 'I saw nothing on Lord Harwich's wrist although I didn't really get a decent look.'

'So, what does it mean?' asked Sabine. 'This man, he's what?'

'He'd have a controlling influence in the group. He's one of the active members,' said Lynn. 'However, I remember Reg saying to me that the groups had created a schism. So, there's more than one. There are two groups, rivals. They were breaking up over, they said, an interpretation of what the Esoteric Tear was. Reg said that was nonsense, and the real reason was a grasp for power. It's like every fundamentalist or religious organisation ever. And most of the secular ones.'

Clarissa stood up. She looked off into the corner of the room for a moment before she strode into the living room. She walked around for a moment and strode back, suddenly aware that everyone's eyes were on her.

'You know what all this means? There could be a war going on for this. There could be a war. Maybe the ones that have it killed Reginald. They were listening to him. Maybe they could get hold of him. I don't know. I don't understand it.'

'But they are probably pretty desperate. They were quite happy to blow his head off. We need to be careful,' said Macleod. 'We need to play this smart. When we go out, we go out in pairs. We make sure where we are going is safe.'

'Well, the first thing we are going to do is talk to Ali Ralston.'

'Well, I need to get back to the station,' said Macleod. 'I can't sit here all day. My absence would be noticed.'

'That's fine. Ali Ralston. Me and Ferguson. Patterson, you stay here with Lynn. Research the book. You're the one that's clued up on the mythology. Find out everything you can, okay?'

Patterson nodded.

'How are we getting back?' asked Macleod. 'I think it's best we leave the car we came in outside.'

'My car's here too,' said Sabine. 'I'll take both of you. Where's your car?' she asked Clarissa.

'It got left on the way up,' said Clarissa. 'Drop the boss off and then we'll go get it before we go to see Ali Ralston.'

They went to leave, but Macleod stopped Clarissa. Seeing

that Patterson had left the table, he drew Clarissa and himself over towards Patterson.

Under his breath he said, 'Now listen up, you're staying here with her. No one else knows about this place except one person, and they're a person I trust emphatically. They're who we've borrowed this place off. You see something you're not happy about, you phone. You see somebody coming towards the door you're not happy about, you get out. Go through the back, get away, phone in and we'll come get you,' said Macleod. 'Treat every person as hostile. Do not answer the door. Am I understood?'

'Very much,' said Patterson.

'Good,' said Macleod.

He turned and walked away to the door, followed closely by Clarissa.

Chapter 15

I t took an hour to drop Macleod off and then head south to pick up Clarissa's car. They made their way back to Inverness, where Clarissa insisted Ferguson drop her car off at the station. From there, they set out to find Ali Ralston.

Scottish Museums were contacted to get a direct number to Ali, but when they couldn't reach her, they were able to contact one of the other touring party. They advised Ali was in the gym. Together Clarissa and Ferguson set off at a pace, arriving at the Inverness gymnasium where Clarissa plodded in wearing her tartan trews and shawl.

'Are you looking to get fit?' asked a man behind a desk.

'I'm looking for someone.'

'You sure you don't want to go for one of our gym memberships?'

'My name's Detective Inspector Clarissa Urquhart. I'm looking for someone. Ali Ralston.'

'Oh yes. I saw her come in. She signed in. I think she's through in one of the boxing gymnasiums.'

'We have special types of gymnasium?' blurted Clarissa.

The man waved at Clarissa, showing the way she should go.'

'We have all sorts,' said the man behind the desk. 'Maybe

you'd like to book in for a trial?'

Clarissa held her hands wide and then pointed her back to herself. 'You think this is a realistic opportunity? You think you're going to sell me a gym membership? No harm in trying, I guess.' She turned and followed Sabine down a few corridors until Sabine stood at a wooden door with small windows cut into it.

'She's in there,' said Sabine. 'Looks to be alone too, on the kick bag.'

'Well then, let's go talk to her.'

Clarissa pushed open the door and found the interior to be fiercely warm. Ali Ralston was sweating buckets, throwing kicks at a bag and then punches. Clarissa thought she looked in superb shape. She consoled herself that she could probably fight dirtier than any of the women who were now in the room, Ferguson included. However, that was because they didn't need to fight dirty.

'Detective Inspector, how are you doing? Do you want to join me?' laughed Ali.

'I'll give it a pass today,' said Clarissa.

'Have you found it?'

'No, it's definitely been on the move though. We're more and more sure that certain parties have gone after it.'

'Certain parties?'

'Yes,' said Clarissa, 'but before I say anything about that, how have you been these last few months? Have you had any offers from anyone to buy the Tear? Have you had any offers from anyone to move it on? Any personal offers for you to steal it?'

'No, no, and well, if the third one was true, I wouldn't be telling you, would I?'

'Probably not,' said Clarissa. 'Always worth a punt. Has

anyone been looking to buy the Tear though?'

'As I said before, I've had a couple of offers. Daft amounts, though. Absolutely daft offers.'

The woman turned and started punching the bag again. Clarissa watched the sweat run down the side of her face. She walked round to the other side of the bag. Rather than punch it, Clarissa put her arm well behind her and swung it round with a hard force that it clattered with a dull thud into the bag. She then took her other arm and did exactly the same.

'He seems a sturdy fellow,' said Clarissa, looking at the bag. 'Tell me, have you had anybody from the Dwellers come to speak to you?'

'Deep worry shot across Ali's face before she could stop it. Anxiety spilled forth. Her hands shook slightly as she hesitated before striking the next blow at the kick bag.'

'Do you know them?' asked Sabine.

'No. No, no, no. Not at all,' said Ali.

'All right. They seem like the sort of people who might have made a big bid. They're tied in with the history of the diamond. Did you know that?'

'I don't think there's a term "Dwellers" in its history.

'The inhabitants, whatever,' said Clarissa. 'The people in the cave. I don't know. Something like that. Certainly, sounds genuine to me.'

'Have you ever heard of a Reginald McLean?' asked Clarissa, as she saw the sweat now pouring off Ali Ralston. That was the thing. Was she sweating because of the punch bag? Clarissa thought not. She thought most of the sweat was now produced by her fear of being caught.

Could she do it, though? Could she get the woman in a position where she'd drop her guard properly so Clarissa could arrest her? Clarissa wasn't sure.

'I don't have an idea what you're talking about,' said Ralston. She punched hard at the bag, left and right.

'It's actually about timing,' said Sabine, 'if I may.'

Clarissa stepped to one side, while Ali Ralston watched the Glasgow-based officer step up to the bag. Sabine was wearing a jacket, and she let it drop to the floor, revealing a tight white top. One foot went in front of the other and Sabine rocked backwards and forwards.

Clarissa nearly dropped when she saw Sabine spend the next minute rapidly hitting the bag, driving fists into it before launching kicks at it.

'That's how you do it. Focus and concentration, back and forward, into it, into it, into it, into it. Doesn't take a lot to learn it. You're doing all right for a beginner.'

Ali Ralston glowered at her, almost wild with fury. 'Like I told you, I haven't seen anyone. Talked to anyone? Certainly not the Dwellers, whoever they are. People make daft bids on items at the museums all the time. Can't remember them all.'

'But there were definitely some?' asked Clarissa.

'Yes, there were.'

'Sheila Alcock's dead, too.'

'I appreciate the punching lesson,' said Ali Ralston, 'but I'm not appreciating the questions. This is my time. I'd like the opportunity to spend a bit of time here, okay?'

'Of course,' said Clarissa. 'Be careful, though. People associated with this case seem to have a habit of dying. I wouldn't want to see it happen to you.'

Clarissa went to the door, and stood there. While the woman was clearly harassed, she was punching the bag but looking everywhere else. There was no focus on what she was doing.

She was just desperate to get out of there. Desperate to be somewhere else.

Sabine followed Clarissa through the door, where they both stopped and looked back in.

'What do you think?' asked Clarissa.

'What do I think? I think,' said Sabine, 'that she's up to her neck in it. I'm not sure what her involvement is, but it can't be good. That I know.'

'Hang on a minute,' said Clarissa. 'She's—she's on the phone.'

The pair stared in, keen not to be caught. But Ali Ralston wasn't looking towards the door. She was looking out of the window, sweat running down her back.

'I wonder who she's talking to,' said Clarissa.

'Well, if you shush, I might hear,' said Sabine.

Clarissa gave a look. 'What's the key thing to do?,' asked Clarissa.

'Follow her.'

'Yes.'

They watched until Ali Ralston came off the phone. She then returned to the kick bag, working hard until four minutes later, she picked up her towel. She started drying herself but stopped short and then headed for the door. Clarissa and Sabine exited quickly, getting back out to the car park before Ali Ralston had even left the building. Once Ali climbed inside her car, Clarissa got ready to tail her.

'You're in your sports car. Are you sure you're going to tail her properly?' asked Sabine. 'I mean, has she seen it before?'

'I'll drop back deep. Don't worry,' said Clarissa.

As Ali Ralston tore out of the car park, Clarissa's phone rang. Sabine answered it.

'How's things going out there?' asked Patterson. 'I've gone

through this manuscript. There are a few interesting points to note. Not everyone in the group seemed to think this thing was real. Some of them just wanted to use it to create the thought in the minds of others. However, in recent years, some of the backers seem to have had difficulty with money. Maybe it's the hard times. So, in recent years, most of their members, although they're not mentioned here, seemed to be recruited from Lords and Ladies. Old money, steeped in history and myth.'

'I'll pass it on,' said Sabine. 'In the meantime, we're seeing where Ali Ralston's going to. We put the squeeze on her, and she's phoned someone, but we're not sure where she's off to.'

'Okay, I'll get on to looking through more of this book with Lynn,' said Patterson. 'I'm not sure what else we'll find. A quick scan usually does it on these things, doesn't it?'

'Devil can be in the details,' said Sabine, feeling a little trite.

Clarissa continued to drive behind Ali Ralston, some distance away, and Sabine was impressed with how the woman could tail someone.

'It takes skill,' Clarissa said. As she drove along, she realised she looked old. Sabine had come in her jacket but revealed underneath it she had some sort of gymnasium top on. Clarissa loved her tartan shawl and trews, but eccentricity never hid your age. At least her outer age, for she didn't feel a day over twenty-one inside.

'Okay,' said Clarissa, 'I think we're close enough behind and besides, she looks like she's pulling over soon.'

'So she is,' said Sabine. Clarissa drove past, parking a little further up the road, where Sabine stepped out of the car quickly. Clarissa followed her.

'There she is,' said Sabine.

'Easy,' said Clarissa, 'we don't want to scare her off. Easy.'
Sabine looked at Clarissa in her tartan clothes and raised an eyebrow.

'Scare her off? You look like you're going to a wedding.'

'Don't you worry about me. I can look normal in any company.'

Flipping cheek, thought Clarissa. *Still, to be expected with the banter I hit Seoras with.*

Chapter 16

Ali Ralston had driven out of Inverness, past the airport, and eventually split off the main road to a place called Findhorn. Driving into Findhorn, Clarissa had parked a distance away but had maintained a long line of sight. Ralston sat in her car for a while, and Clarissa watched along with Sabine. Eventually, she sent Sabine out to walk round the town and try to spot anyone approaching.

Via text, Sabine reported seeing no one, and soon Ali got out of the car. Someone drove past Clarissa and parked up close to Ali. He stepped out of the car. It was a black-haired man in the early part of his middle age, maybe just past thirty. He looked reasonably well built but had a sly disposition.

Ali walked up to him, embraced him, and kissed him passionately. Stepping away from him, the two spoke for a few moments. The man's face seemed to become angry. He fired some questions at Ali, clearly accusatory but not loud.

Clarissa watched as Ali gave a response and was then slapped hard across the cheek. Clarissa thought if it was she who received that slap, the man in front of her wouldn't be standing. She'd have obliterated him. But Ali didn't. Instead, she was almost submissive, taking her punishment. Clarissa wondered what sort of relationship this was.

They continued to talk, arguing occasionally. Clarissa stared at the conversation through her binoculars from the car. She scanned the man up and down, seeing his normal everyday jeans and regular boots. Everything about him was indistinct. And then he held a fist up to Ali, showing the inside of his wrist. Clarissa thought she saw a design. Was that a tattoo? Was that design the same as the one Macleod had seen on Lord Harwich's bodyguard?

Clarissa picked up her phone and called Sabine. The woman had a small backpack with her, with a long lens camera.

'Sabine, I think I can see something on the man's wrist. I don't know if you can. Can you get in a position to get a photograph of it? My phone won't be able to reach that far. We'll need the big lens. You might need to hide out. Hopefully, he'll keep talking.'

'Will do. But it won't be that easy to take a shot from this distance. I can't get too close. It'll be obvious with the big lens.'

'Whatever you're going to do, do it quick,' said Clarissa. 'I don't know how long this argument's going to continue.'

Clarissa put her binoculars back up and saw the man berating Ali. Ali opened her arms wide, shaking her head. The man then indicated something small. Was he talking about the diamond? Did Ali have the diamond? Were they looking for the diamond? What on earth was going on?

Clarissa was struggling because she couldn't get a handle on just who was doing what. Ali Ralston was clearly involved, somehow, in the disappearance. But had she been stolen from? Or had she been the one to take part in the theft?

Clarissa mused on whether she should bring her into the station and formerly interview her. But she had so little to go on. And if Ali clammed up, they wouldn't get anywhere. This man, however, clearly was part of a bigger connection. Was he a Dweller? Did he believe in the gem and its power? He certainly seemed to be part of the hierarchy. A deacon maybe, one of the operators in the society. Or was it a cult? Well, maybe he'd stolen it, or was organising getting it back. That would account for his presence, wouldn't it?

That would make sense. After all, one side must be trying to get it back. Reginald had said there was a schism dividing the group in two. While the museum had the gem, both sides would try to get it. But now somebody had it. Maybe both sides were vying for it. Ali had arranged originally to hand over the gem at some point, and that's why this man was so angry. *Good theories, old girl, but no evidence.*

Her phone vibrated, and she looked down. Ferguson had messaged to say she'd got the shot. Did Clarissa want her to return to the car?

'I think so,' messaged Clarissa.

Clarissa watched the argument ahead of her on the street continue. As Clarissa continued to sit, she saw Sabine Ferguson sliding in behind the car, clocking her in the rear-view mirror. Smoothly, the tall Northern Irish woman slid into the passenger seat and then threw her rucksack into the backseat. She turned and reached round, picked out the camera and then whipped the memory card from it. She attached that to a small tablet she pulled from the bag. With it, she messaged the station, sending the photograph off for an examination.

'Good,' said Clarissa, 'at least we've got something.'

'They started out lovey-dovey, didn't they?' said Sabine. 'Then it got heated.'

'I was trying to guess what sort of relationship they had,' said

Clarissa. 'Is he dominating her? Is she just a pawn? I'm not sure.'

'Seems strange though, doesn't it? You saw her kickboxing,' said Sabine. 'I know I gave her a bit of a lesson, but to be honest, she can handle herself. If somebody slapped me like that, I'd have slapped them back.'

'She's gentler than I am,' said Clarissa.

'So I've heard,' said Sabine. Clarissa raised her eyebrows, but then stared back at the couple.

'How long do you think they're going to go on for? They seem to be having a right good conversation about it.'

'I think they're worried. They're definitely worried. Wouldn't you be,' said Sabine. 'Assuming she's taken the stone, you would be worried because somebody's coming after you. We've turned up to talk to her.'

'But that's not unusual,' said Clarissa. 'She lost it so we would turn up to talk to her. Of course we would.'

'It doesn't stop you getting worried though,' said Sabine. 'Doesn't stop you sitting there thinking they're on to me. If she hasn't taken it, maybe she's worried that someone else has. Maybe she was going to give it to someone before it was taken.'

'Crossed my mind, too,' said Clarissa.

'Oh, look,' said Sabine. 'They're splitting up. We want to follow one of them. I haven't got my car here or we could go after them both.'

'Ali Ralston isn't going anywhere,' said Clarissa. 'She's got her job to do. If she wants to maintain cover, she'll stay local. If she's stolen the diamond, she knows where it is. There's no need to run. After all, if she disappears at the moment, she's just told us she's guilty. If she hasn't, then she needs to tag in with us to get it back. Find out what we know and what anybody else knows.

'For the moment, Ali Ralston's going nowhere. That man, however, we don't even know who he is, and we don't know where he's going to go. What we know is he's part of the group. Certainly, one side of them. So, we need to find out more about him. We need to see where he goes.'

'Well, we're decided then,' said Sabine.

They sat as the man got back into his car. He didn't disappear immediately, instead letting Ali Ralston drive away first. The man sat there for another ten minutes before he departed. Meanwhile, the station had come back. They hadn't come up with any names as the check they'd put through was unsuccessful.

'Now we really need to tail him,' said Sabine.

The car drove away, and Clarissa spun the little green car out approximately thirty seconds later. She maintained her distance, Sabine still deeply impressed by how she could covertly tail anyone in the car she was using. They headed back towards Inverness in what seemed a wandering pattern on reaching the city. When Clarissa received a call on her phone, she activated the hands-free.

'I see you've sent me a photograph,' said Macleod.

'He's also got a tattoo the same as the other man,' said Clarissa in answer. 'We're on his tail at the moment, currently back in Inverness. I'm not sure where he's going.'

'Well, don't lose him,' said Macleod. 'Whatever you do, stay on him.'

'Well, funny enough, you talking to me on the phone just makes it all that much easier. Especially the support and encouragement that's coming through.'

'Don't be facetious,' said Macleod. 'Anyway, I talked to

Patterson. He's not coming up with much more from our intrepid editor. However, they are safe.'

'Well, at least the last time you spoke to him, they were. Hang on a minute, Seoras.'

The man pulled up in his car, outside a lockup, and disappeared inside for a moment before he walked away.

'Seoras, we're going to have to go. He's pulled up outside a lockup and I need to get in there. I think I can do it quickly enough.'

'Have you got any—'

'Don't, don't, and don't,' said Clarissa. 'If I find anything of use, I will come back in here with some proper reason.'

'I am not listening to you,' said Macleod, thankful the line wasn't recorded.

Clarissa closed down the call without even a goodbye.

'Sabine, get out and tail him. I want at least a thirty-second warning to get the heck out of there when he's coming back. You understand me?'

Sabine nodded, jumped out of the car as she pulled her jacket on and followed the man. Clarissa stepped out of the car and walked over to the lockup. She bent down to look at the lock in front of her.

One thing about hiding stuff was to make sure you didn't hide it somewhere that looked like something was being hidden. The lockup just looked like anyone's basic garage. The lock attached at the bottom of the roller shutters was flimsy, to say the least. Clarissa reckoned the key mechanism wasn't much cop.

Looking inside her shawl, Clarissa pulled out a small set of lock pick keys. She'd been experimenting with them, never really intending to use them during a case. But at the moment, with two dead and her case on the line, she would not hang about.

Bending down, she fiddled. The lock didn't budge. *Bugger*, she thought. She picked up the lock keys and went back to sit in the car. *Had she done that bit right?* She returned to the door, got down on her knees again and worked the lock. Five minutes later, it came apart.

She was able to push up the shutters though they were stiff. She left the lock just inside, pulled the shutters back down, and then turned around, activating the light on the back of her phone. In front of her stood an item that caused Clarissa to gasp in shock.

Chapter 17

larissa's eyes narrowed as she stared at a motorbike she had seen before. The markings were the same; the colour was the same. This was owned by the man she had faced down. She had taken him on after she had dropped Patterson off to collect the jewels when they had been thrown from the motorbike. She was in the right place.

So, Ali Ralston was an accomplice to this. Whoever this man was, she had let him take the jewels. That must have been it. Or why would they be here, in her associate's lockup? Clarissa had doubted she'd find anything, but it was now more than a promising lead.

The lockup was a bit of a mess. Yes, there was a motorbike standing in the middle of it, a bike she recognised, but around it was junk. Clearly the bike had to get in and out quickly and that's why it was positioned so centrally with such an obvious clear route to the door.

She turned and started looking along the wall. Several sheets covered items, and Clarissa lifted them up gently, looking underneath. There were a couple of tea chests that she lifted the lids off. Her fingers got covered in a grimy dust, but she ignored that, instead looking inside. There were nails, a collection of picture frames, a piece of metal she wasn't sure what it was for, and various other bits of junk.

She re-covered it all with the sheets and sidled down to lift another sheet and see a load of motorbike parts. There was a large, coiled spring, but she ignored it, looking around for somewhere you would keep something precious. There were several tins on the shelf and she opened the first one, peering inside. She lifted it to her nose. *Tea? Was that tea? Old tea?*

She put her hand inside and it may have been tea because she couldn't find anything else. She took her hand out and saw that the tea had mixed with the grimy dust her hands had been on before. Clarissa was going to leave a trail if she wasn't careful.

Reluctantly, she lifted her shawl, took the underside of it and wiped her hands on it. It would have to hit the wash. No, the dry cleaner. This shawl was, well, it was part of her, wasn't it? She couldn't get it too dirty. It came out every winter. She had the lighter one for summer, if indeed she needed one. Oh, Macleod would pay the dry-cleaning bill. That was one thing she'd make sure of.

Clarissa moved on round, lifting boxes, peering inside, but there was no diamond, no jewel hidden away. She moved across to the other side of the lockup and found a book, which she flipped open. Places were written. Names, too. But only first names. Not even an initial afterward. There were various times written too, but none of the times were related to a place and there were no calendar dates written either.

Clarissa lifted out her phone and photographed the book. She wasn't sure it would mean anything. Maybe afterwards. Sometimes evidence like this came in to its own at the end of an investigation. Supporting evidence. Once you knew who the real culprits were, it was additional evidence. Maybe that's how it would work. She wasn't sure, but it was worth taking. How long had it been, though? Had she been in here long?

Clarissa had the shutter down but there was a window high on the left-hand side which was giving her light. She had decided not to switch on the light, which hung simply in the middle of the garage. Lifting up another cloth, she found mats underneath. A bicycle was on the far side. A man's bicycle, well, a racer certainly. Although, by all means, you could see a woman on it. *Not this woman, though*, thought Clarissa. She didn't do bikes. Cars were her thing.

Her phone vibrated, and Clarissa answered the call, seeing it was Ferguson.

'He's made a phone call. We've walked some distance away,' she said. 'And he popped into a house too, possibly his own. Not sure. He had a key for it, certainly. And he's made his way back now towards the lockup. I reckon you've maybe got three to four minutes, tops. You'd best get out.'

Clarissa thanked Ferguson for the information, put her phone away and turned back to the shutter door of the lockup. She reached down and went to pull it up. It lifted, maybe a few inches, and then stopped. *What on earth?* she thought to herself. She reached down and pulled again.

In her head, Clarissa was counting. A couple of minutes, Ferguson said. Clarissa was stuck and struggling to know what to do next. Reaching down, she pulled with all her might. Something was jamming the shutter door. *I'd better sort myself out*, Clarissa thought. But there was meant to be a lock on the shutter, wasn't there?

Clarissa went to the corner of the shutter door and looked down, seeing where the loop came through to lock the shutter.

She didn't have a choice. She took the padlock sitting just inside the shutter where she'd left it. Carefully, she let it sit just inside the loop, hoping that the man would think it had sprung back open.

Had he tested it? She wasn't sure. It was an old lock and not a good one. She might get away with it. She let it sit, ever so gently, on the edge of the loop that it should have gone through. He'd better think it had sprung back.

Clarissa pulled her arm back out, stood up opposite the shutter door and pushed down. It went down with a clatter. She then looked around her. Hiding was now a necessity but where?

She went over to where the bicycle was. Lifting the sheet that was there, she clambered underneath behind the bike, before dropping the sheet down. Her knees were up to her chin. Her arms could barely move. If somebody opened the sheet up, what would she do. She'd have to shove the bike at him and hope for the best.

Reaching underneath her shawl for her phone, she checked it was on silent, and switched the vibration off as well. She then sent a quick text to Ferguson. *I'm trapped. I have to wait this out. Be close by in case he finds me. I may need assistance.*

Clarissa waited in the dark. She'd been able to see inside the lockup because of the window, but now she was behind a sheet, and it really was a much darker view. As she waited, she was still producing a count in her head.

It had been four minutes since Ferguson had called, and then she heard footsteps approaching. There was a grunt outside the shutter door.

'Bloody piss-poor lock,' said a voice. 'Look at that. Need to lock this up better. Thank goodness there's no important crap here.'

The shutter door was suddenly pushed up. Clarissa wondered why she couldn't shift it. Could have been jammed on the outside? She wasn't sure, and right now it didn't really matter. She heard someone step in and the shutter door went down behind them.

'Right then,' said a voice. 'I suppose I better call her.'

Clarissa wasn't able to see anything, but she imagined a phone being taken out and a call being placed. The interior of the lockup was deadly quiet, and she tried not to breathe loudly, instead trying to quietly draw her breaths in and out through her nose. Every time she did though, she thought it sounded like someone having their last breath, dragging out painfully through their lungs. The man didn't seem to notice though as he suddenly spoke into the phone.

'Ali, we're go for tonight. We're going to meet the society. Yes, I told you it would work. You'll get your money, don't worry. We'll do the handover, but they want us both there'—there was a moment's silence—'Well, I think they want us both there because, at the end of the day, they want to see who they're dealing with. They're going to want to know you'll stay quiet. It'll be fine. They'll get what they want, you'll get your money, that'll be it. And then we'll clear off, okay?'—more silence—'It won't be a problem. Just chill, okay? I don't care if they were snooping around. Anyway, the old girl's likely to get a hernia if she breaks out of a walk.'

Clarissa's hand clenched. *This old girl feels like getting up and throwing this bike into your head,* thought Clarissa. She felt her shoulder twinge with the mention of the old girl. She owed him one, and she'd give him a good kick for it. But now wasn't the time.

'I don't think they've trailed you. And I don't think they've trailed me, okay? Tonight. Loch Garten's where we're going. They'll be there; it won't be a problem. Then you and I will walk off with a bit of money. Okay? No, I don't think it's the real thing. I mean seriously. We'll be made though. I've told them to bring it in cash. There'll be two suitcases. You take one and I take the other. We'll be made.'

Clarissa made a mental note. Loch Garten wasn't that far away. She wondered if she'd get a time for the meeting.

'It'll be dark. Pitch black by the time we get there. I'll come and pick you up, though. That'll be the best thing. I'll meet you on the way out of Inverness. That Information place that used to be on the way out. It's a cafe now, isn't it? That'll be shut. I'll meet you in the car park in there. You hide behind the trees. Loads of people leave their cars there at night. You go out for a walk, couples go in for a, well, you know, and you and me will have the money. We'll clear off then. Or, well, if you want, we could continue some of what we've done.'

Now that's interesting, thought Clarissa. *They aren't just partners in crime; they are actually seeing each other.*

'I'm going to get some stuff sorted. Need some food anyway. I'll see you there tonight, okay? Don't be late.'

Clarissa heard the man turn and then the shutter door went flying up. She heard him walk back a few steps, and the bike was wheeled out. The door was shut again.

She thought that the lock might have been put back in place. Clarissa didn't move. She heard the bike roar and then it disappeared off. Clarissa was trapped if he'd locked it from the outside. She threw off the sheet in front of the bicycle, pushed the bike forward, and clambered out of her position.

Her knees ached. She hadn't been balled up that tight in a

long while, but she put the sheet back over the bike and tried to leave everything as it was. The diamond wasn't here. He'd said so. The motorbike was gone. She'd just have to get out.

She walked to the lockup door and tried to lift it, but this time it didn't even move more than a half an inch. He'd put the padlock back on, hadn't he? Clarissa sat down on her bottom, looking at the door. *Bugger*, she thought. She placed a call, but no one was answering. Had Ferguson disappeared off after him? Surely not.

'Oh, come on,' she said out loud and then stopped herself. No, she'd need to stay quiet. Maybe he'd come back. Maybe there were other people that used this lockup. She'd have a chance to hide, though. They'd need to undo the lock. That would give her a moment. She looked around her, but found nothing. Ten minutes later, she was wondering how she could get back out. Could she force it? The lock wasn't great, was it? It really wasn't.

Footsteps were coming towards her. Somebody was then fiddling with the lock. Clarissa moved quickly, throwing up the sheet which was over the bicycle, clambered in behind it, and pulled the sheet back down. It was about a minute later when the shutter door flew up. Someone stepped inside, looking around. Then there came a quiet voice, but in a very Northern Irish accent.

'Clarissa, you there? Did you haul yourself in here and not get out?'

It was Ferguson. Clarissa pushed the sheet which dropped, revealing the bike holding her inside. Ferguson turned round and moved the shutter about halfway down. She pulled the bike away then from Clarissa, helping her up to her feet, and placed the bike back.

145

'Sorry, I've lost him. I thought I'd better come and find you. I had heard nothing, so I just wanted to make sure you were safe. But I've lost him. Like Macleod paraphrased, your safety was paramount, though.'

'Come on,' said Clarissa. She threw the shutter up, giving the mechanism a stare on either side, wondering why things hadn't worked for her before. Then she closed it down and put the lock back on. The two women then walked back to their car.

'Lock picks then,' Clarissa said to Ferguson.

'Absolutely. You know how it is. You've got to know how to do a lock.'

'Well done,' she said.

'But I've lost him. Do you know who he is?'

'No,' said Clarissa. 'But he's heading out tonight with Ali Ralston. At least, I think he is. Sounded like it from the way he talked on the phone. And he's meeting her tonight. Then, they're meeting the Society, whoever that is, out at Loch Garten. He's going to meet her up at the little cafe on the way out of Inverness back down the A9. The one at the very top of the hill.'

Ferguson smiled. 'I made the right choice then.'

'Even if I was okay, you made the right choice,' said Clarissa, 'especially with the way this case is. Macleod's right. We need to keep an eye on each other. No diamond's worth us.'

'I'm glad to hear it,' said Ferguson. 'I certainly don't intend to die soon. So, if you want me to stay alive, I'll do my very best.'

'Let's go talk to the boss. Get ourselves set up for tonight,' said Clarissa. 'I think we're getting somewhere. I finally think we're getting somewhere.'

Chapter 18

Clarissa watched the kettle boil in the small house at Culloden Moor. Macleod was due to arrive any minute, but he'd be making his way in quietly. Patterson was sitting at the table, along with Lynn Green. All over the table were bits and pieces of paper, notes that Patterson had made.

He'd really gone into this, which had impressed Clarissa. He wasn't au fait with the arts world, but on one hand, this wasn't quite the usual arts case. For a change, they were looking into the mythology, looking to understand these zealots. It made a change from looking at the business side, items stolen simply for their monetary value. Here, they were chasing people who had rather far-fetched beliefs.

Beliefs of this sort were not uncommon, historically speaking. Notre Dame, after all, had been funded by the Templars and packed with references and symbols. People had put symbology all over items, all over buildings throughout history. In the modern age, there was a school of thought that people believed nothing that seemed daft, that seemed crazy. Some people talked about religions being myths in the sense of stories, just fables, having no reality to them.

Mythology, of course, was something that shouldn't be judged by historical accuracy. It was the tales of a culture. But the truth of the tales, that was another story. Mythology just recounted the stories. In the arts world, you needed to understand the mythology. *Mythology and history*, thought Clarissa as she put some instant coffee into a cup.

She stopped, thinking about Macleod arriving. He wouldn't be happy with this coffee. He'd have to make do. Maybe that would be the giveaway if somebody broke into the house though. Oh look, it's proper coffee. This must be where Macleod keeps them.

She laughed to herself. But then she drew a breath as she heard the front door open and then close with a shout of, 'it's Seoras.' At least it wasn't anyone else.

She poured the water into the cup and continued to fill two more cups, before lifting them onto a tray. Clarissa carefully carried it into the dining room. Macleod had already seated himself behind the table. Ferguson was close to him, whereas Lynn Green had shuffled up close to Patterson, leaving Clarissa almost on the other side on her own.

One thing about being the boss, although she knew she wasn't the overall boss, was that everybody seemed to edge away from you when you sat down for meetings. She hadn't remembered that when she'd been in Hope's office, or indeed Macleod's little office, when she'd been on the murder team. He could sit close to everyone, or did he? Or was it just that Als beside him, so it didn't look the same?

'And what's this?' asked Macleod, as she put a cup of black coffee in front of him. 'Instant?'

'We're all making sacrifices. Just drink it.'

'A cup of water would be better,' he said. She scowled at him, but then saw his wry smile.

'Don't,' said Clarissa. 'Just don't. Okay? In the middle of a case, the big boss, that's you, you're meant to be gentle and boost us.'

'You don't need a boost, Clarissa,' said Macleod, quietly.

She looked at him. 'What's that meant to mean?'

'You've got this,' he said. 'Teeth are in and you will not let go. I can sense it.'

She sat down as a quiet descended over the table. Patterson was conveniently looking at a piece of paper, whereas Ferguson seemed deeply interested in some random picture on the wall. Lynn Green just looked confused.

'Right, let's get the discussion going again,' said Clarissa. 'After that, rather obscure—well, let's just move on.' She glanced back at Macleod, who still had the wry smile on.

'We know what's happening tonight,' said Clarissa. 'We can't identify our contact, but he is clearly having some sort of relationship with Ali Ralston, and along with her, stole the Esoteric Tear. They're obviously trying to sell it on, so they're meeting up with the buyers tonight, expecting to get paid. They're meeting up first of all at the little coffee stop on the way out of Inverness, the one that used to be the information centre, when it's dark. Following that, they're off to Loch Garten. We'll need to cover both off.'

'I think we should surround the place,' said Macleod. 'See who turns up, sweep in, grab them all.'

'No,' said Clarissa.

'And why not?' asked Macleod. 'It'll get the diamond back.'

'Because it won't end there, will it? The diamond will appear again, and people will go after it again. And what are you going to charge them with? We're not the secret service who can close them down unofficially. The only people we're going to get with this,' said Clarissa, 'are Ali Ralston and her man. Making further charges will be difficult if these people have real clout in society.'

'How many people do you need to get?' asked Macleod.

'Them all,' said Ferguson. 'We need to get them all. This item, it's like a talisman. It's not something that you're going to hand back to the museums and that's going to be it. We need to get into this society and break it up. We also want to trace them back. Find out who killed Reginald. Find out who killed Sheila Alcock. We need to go right back on this. There are people who are operating rather dangerously. Well, taking the diamond out of circulation and putting it back in the museum isn't going to deal with that.'

'I hope it might,' said Macleod, 'because I'm not sure how well we're going to link through any of these murders. The killing of Reginald is pretty clean. I'm not getting anything concrete from down south. They're struggling. Sheila Alcock, not a lot coming from that investigation either.'

'But that's the point, isn't it?' said Clarissa. 'We need to hit some people at the top. We need to know where this diamond is going. Need to track it through. If they purchased it knowing it was stolen, we could get them for that. We may even link something through from it. I don't know, but Ali Ralston and her man are small fry.'

'We're clutching at straws a bit,' said Macleod. 'Safer to just grab everyone.'

Clarissa looked away for a moment.

'I agree with Clarissa,' said Sabine. 'We need to go up this chain.'

All eyes turned towards Patterson for a moment. 'I think we

need to look at the big picture here. If we follow to the meeting, we can identify anyone attending. Sure, if we catch them with the item, we might secure convictions. But we could also push back through the layers on the quiet. We've got two sides,' said Patterson. 'We may be able to get one side to drop the other into it. I think we need to understand the numbers involved before we wrap this up too quickly.'

'If this goes up high, it might be difficult to secure those convictions,' said Macleod. 'What's the safest way to do this without more people getting killed? That's my primary concern,' he said. 'Professional contract killing on a man who wrote a book about a diamond that opens a portal at the end of times. These people are killing for the daftest of reasons,'

Clarissa stood up, pushing herself to that position with hands on the table, tutting as she did so.

'Seoras, would you listen to me? It's the damn arts world. Okay, these people are believers. These people actually, well some of them, think this gem is a piece of magic. There are others who realise that the nutters who think that are going to pay big bucks for the item. But they also want to make sure, these nutters, that they're not stopped. We have to stop the influence. There'll be people up at the top of this. Harwich is involved. Don't ask me how, but he'll pull big strings. You tell me you just want to let him swan around?'

'I don't want to let anyone swan around,' said Macleod. 'But I'm looking at the overall here. It's an arts investigation and we have two people dead. They're not accidentally killed. Two people murdered just because they were involved. What I don't want to do is keep pushing this and we end up with a trail of bodies all the way back. I've got another team for that. I need to hit the source. I'm not having a pile of dead bodies over what? Some jewel that means nothing.'

'Some jewel that means everything to them,' said Clarissa. 'You want to stop the bodies? We need to get to the top. Because they'll go after this and keep going after it until we do.'

'It's your call,' said Macleod. 'It's your call, but just be warned. Things get out of control—I bring everything in. I just call a halt.'

'Did you have anyone ever call a halt on you?' spat Clarissa.

'I knew when to stop, when to call a halt,' said Macleod, 'and I was working on murder cases. That there might be some bodies along the way was kind of taken for granted.'

'Well, I say we go for this. I say we get right up to the top. Reginald died for nothing—to be silenced—and I want to find out who did it.'

'And so do I,' said Macleod, 'but make sure we don't sacrifice others on the way.'

'If I can just interject,' said Patterson. Everyone at the table turned to look at him. 'We're getting very hyped up about what we're going to do, but now that Clarissa's called it, let's recap what we've got. I want everyone to be aware of what we're looking at.

'The Esoteric *T-air*, as in rip, not *T-ear* as in water from your eyes, is a jewel that is believed to be of assistance in the end times. It may look a bit like a tear but it's not, it's a *T-air*. It will open up the fabric of reality to keep you safe during a time when everything is falling apart. Having gone through the book and other information I've found on the net, that time is close. Their believed time for this happening is close, therefore they will step up what they are going to do.

'So Seoras, I'm totally in agreement with Clarissa. We need

to put an end to this. If you put it somewhere safe, they'll take it back forcibly, or maybe in a deadly manner. I could not get any names, but from what is said in the book, you have several positions. Deacons, other ranks best described as elders, acolytes. It's a small group, but it's got some powerful figures in it. It doesn't say who, but the ability to manipulate at the government level, the ability to manipulate within the force. I do not recommend giving out Lynn's position until we secure these people. Once we've done that, whatever she says will be irrelevant. There'll be no names to give.'

'I haven't got names to give,' said Lynn.

'But they believe you do,' said Patterson, 'clearly. Reginald was right when he talks about them being like modern-day Knights Templar. They're in there influencing everything. I would suggest we trust no one.'

'No one?' said Macleod suddenly. 'When you say no one, are you talking about my assistant chief constable as well?'

'No one!' said Patterson.

'I've known Jim for ages, though. He's incredibly helpful.'

'But that's the point,' said Patterson suddenly. 'That's what they do. They look normal, and in most things in life, they are following a very genuine thread. Just say our assistant chief constable was one. He would help you with the normal everyday things of controlling crime, investigating, dealing with murderers. But this is something different. This is talking about an end time he would see as inevitable, and one that is coming soon.'

'Is there anywhere on the web you could trace these people through?' said Macleod. 'Nutters like this broadcast what they have to say.'

'Not this group,' said Patterson. 'This group will stay in the shadows. This group will do nothing. They didn't even come and steal the item themselves. They've got somebody else to do it.'

'But he is part of the group,' said Clarissa. 'The man on the bike had a tattoo. He's a deacon in the group.'

'Maybe that's how the contact was made with Ali Ralston,' said Macleod.

'Maybe,' said Sabine. 'Or maybe she's got nothing to do with it except stealing it for a bit of the money. She said it wasn't worth anything. Maybe she believes it isn't. Maybe she just believes in the money.'

'She might have been taken in by him, though,' said Clarissa. 'There was that sort of romantic aspect. Either way, we'll follow this through. We'll keep eyes on. We'll swoop when we're ready. And only when we get higher up the chain, for we need to see who's involved. Who really are the players?

'I'm going to need everybody, though,' said Clarissa. 'So, how does this work? We're not going to leave Lynn here on her own.'

'I'll come over,' said Macleod. 'I'll come over. Jane will cover for me at the house.'

'What if you get dragged out on a murder with the other team? You do work across several teams.'

'If so, I'll fob Hope off with something. She can run a murder investigation in the meantime. When you'll be back by dawn, it won't be a problem.'

'Good,' said Clarissa, 'because I need Sabine and I need Pats. Then, hopefully, we won't be too long.

'It is getting a bit cooped up in here,' said Lynn.

'It's for your own safety,' said Sabine. 'Trust me.'

Lynn nodded, but the frustration of having to remain within

the safe house was clearly showing.

'So that's that,' said Clarissa. 'Let's get some food, and then we'll get out there. I'll work with Pats tonight. Sabine, you'll be in the spare car. We'll do the close surveillance; you'll be the backup.'

'And if it all goes wrong,' said Macleod, 'I call it. You call me and I'll call it. Everyone will come. The first sign that we look in trouble, don't hesitate. I'm not about to lose officers as well.'

Clarissa nodded, and Macleod stood up from behind the desk.

'I'll get off now,' he said, 'but I'll be back in a couple of hours. I'll need to explain to Jane what I'm doing so she can cover for me. Don't worry, I won't tell her where this is.'

He disappeared off out the door. Patterson came up close to Clarissa, whispering quietly, 'Are you sure about this? I know we need to find the people at the top. Should we not expand the team?'

'We've got it, Pats. We've got it, trust me. Working with less gives you the freedom to do more.'

Chapter 19

Clarissa was dressed in green. It was a tartan shawl, but it was the hunting tartan—a pattern of greens with the occasional red and black. She played fast and loose often with the tartan she wore. It didn't have to be from the family, after all. Yes, she was an Urquhart, and she was proud of it, but didn't have to be that way. She had plenty others along the family line, other clans she could drop into and ultimately, if she just liked the look of a tartan, she'd have it.

Not the Macleod tartan though. She didn't particularly like the Macleod tartan beforehand. Now she felt it justified her being called Macleod's Rottweiler.

As she lay down in the grass, trees around her, watching the car park at Loch Garten, Clarissa pondered on Macleod, calling her his Rottweiler. He never really said it to her. It had been something other people had said, as if he had her on some sort of leash and let her off.

They didn't say that about Hope. Hope, who was now the detective inspector running the murder team, and a long-time colleague of Macleod's, didn't get described as a Rottweiler. In fairness, Hope was younger. She was attractive, six feet tall, long, red hair, and had a body that, Clarissa understood, would certainly turn a few men's heads.

She was the consummate police officer as well, very well spoken, thorough, professional, and dogged. She could handle herself when things got physical, for she could fight. But she would apprehend people professionally too, bringing them down with the minimum of effort, trying not to hurt them.

Clarissa wasn't that strong, and she was a lot older. She'd grown up in a force where there weren't so many women, and certainly not so many women in leading positions. Clarissa had learned to fight dirty on lots of different fronts: physically, mentally, for promotions. She remembered being spurned for some of them just because there was a man, probably of lesser ability, picked out by the boys.

Clarissa had never been anti-man. She was no feminist. But she agreed that the force had come a long way. She'd had to fight like a man, and they never really accepted her. So, she'd had to be tougher. But Rottweiler. Why was he saying Rottweiler?

Macleod had asked her into the murder squad. She'd wondered why she was there. She'd thought at first he just needed someone quite tough. Clarissa had seen Hope as someone who didn't get that extra out of suspects. In truth, having Clarissa there had probably saved Macleod's life during the time they'd taken him.

Clarissa hadn't been working, was off medically and yet she'd gone in, found Macleod who'd been kidnapped, and rescued him. He was a colleague, so you didn't go by the book when he was under threat. That was the thing about Hope. She would try, and try hard, but she wouldn't have done what Clarissa had done.

157

Macleod couldn't turn round and sanction it afterwards. Jim, the Assistant Chief Constable, couldn't either. He'd officially given her a warning and told her she wasn't to do anything like that again. She was lucky to still be on the force.

Macleod had rewarded her with the arts job. Jim had taken her into Macleod's office one day and just pointed across the desk at him, telling Clarissa the reward was right there. Of course, Jim had sanctioned her moving up into the arts. And yet here she was, lying out amongst a lot of trees, watching a car park in the middle of nowhere.

Loch Garten was between the Boat of Garten and Nethy Bridge, on the way out towards Aviemore. You took an exit and got out into what was really the Highlands. She loved living up here, especially in the open air. Though she was lying down on uncomfortable terrain with a set of binoculars watching a car park as darkness was falling, she was enjoying herself. She really was.

She wasn't so sure about Patterson. He'd had to get a change of clothing and was now wearing some jeans and a proper jumper. He wasn't built for the outdoors, she was sure. Ferguson was wearing what Clarissa thought were things you would wear to the gym. The trousers didn't seem to have that many pockets on them. She had a belt which stored away her items.

Clarissa was aware the three of them were very different. There were a couple of others on the Arts team she may link in closer with in the time to come, but for the moment, she was glad she'd brought Sabine in. She reminded her of Hope. Tall, pretty good-looking but Sabine might be prepared to go a little off piste in an investigation. Patterson, he was maybe more by the book, but he was seeing the big picture and seeing it well. So much so he was telling Macleod what they had to do. Yes, the team was a good one.

A text message came in from Ferguson advising that the motorbike man had picked up Ali Ralston and they were heading down towards Loch Garten. Ferguson was following at a distance and didn't think she'd been spotted. Clarissa's little green sports car was carefully hiding away in one part of the car park. It wasn't an extensive car park and there were a couple of cars there. People would sometimes park up here, go off on a wander, spend several days camping out and come back to it. It wasn't strange to find cars sitting in places like this for a while.

She looked over at where Patterson was sitting. She couldn't see him. That was good. At least he was getting the idea. Clarissa sat and thought through more about her team as a motorbike pulled into the car park. It was truly dark now. The single beam from the front of the bike lighting up the car park until it stopped. The engine went off, and a torch came on.

Clarissa could see the outline of a woman on the back of the bike, assuming it was Ralston. She texted Ferguson, telling her to remain a little way off. And Clarissa waited.

Ali Ralston and the man walked out of the car park and over towards the shore of Loch Garten. Carefully, Clarissa made her way through the trees and the undergrowth, crossing the road quickly when the pair had crossed it. She took up a new position in the shadows, watching through binoculars.

Clarissa wasn't that close, but she didn't want to get too close. She didn't want to be stumbled upon by whoever they were meeting. No car was here, so maybe the man had come on foot that would meet them or indeed the woman.

It was another hour with the occasional chatter between

Ralston and her driver until a figure emerged from the shadows. It was wearing a hood and Clarissa couldn't see the face in the darkness. A torch was shone on Ralston and the motorcycle rider. A few words were muttered beyond the hearing of Clarissa before two hoods were produced. They were put over the motorcyclist and Ali Ralston.

Clarissa watched as the pair held hands with the man behind them placing a hand on each exterior shoulder. Slowly he walked them back to the roadside where they stood awaiting someone. Clarissa messaged Patterson, telling him to be ready to move and advising that the trio looked like they were waiting for a pickup. When it didn't arrive within the next couple of minutes, Clarissa tried to get closer, and as she did so, she could hear some of what was being said.

'It'll be here in a few minutes.' It was a male voice that came from the hooded figure, deep, almost growling.

'What's your name?' asked Ali Ralston.

'My name is unimportant. I am taking you to the one you have made the agreement with. When we get there, the exchange will happen.'

'And afterwards?' asked Ali.

'Afterwards, you'll be returned here. You'll be free to go with your money. Don't panic. It's all under control. But we have to maintain secrecy,' said the man. 'I'm sure you understand that.'

Ali Ralston may have understood it but Clarissa could see she was shaking. Clearly, she wasn't used to this type of thing.

In her time, Clarissa had witnessed several exchanges, usually of contraband goods. And she'd realised that there were different types of people who did this sort of thing. There were those who were confident about it. Measurably confident.

In fact, they were born to it. They would casually stroll into the situation, not breaking a sweat. Nerves didn't seem to come across their face. They were professional, understanding what was happening, knowing what to look for.

There were those who understood what to look for, but were still nervous, and couldn't hide the tension. They put on a facade, but really, underneath, they were being cut to the core. She always wondered why these sorts of people even got involved in doing this type of action. Maybe it was because the money was so good. Everyone had a reason, everybody had a sick child or a mortgage that need paid, or just wanted to be fabulously rich and get out of that day job.

Whatever it was, the people that did it were shaking to the core when they did it despite understanding what was happening. These were the ones that troubled Clarissa because these were the ones that usually went wrong for her. The motorcycle rider was clearly nervous. He was one of these people. Ali Ralston, Clarissa thought, has not done this before. She was nervous, jabbering.

'And your group, will all your group be there?'

'You shall see soon enough,' said the man. 'I appreciate you may not be used to these activities and our secrecy, but trust me, Miss Ralston, it's necessary.'

'I just don't like not knowing your name, and it's boiling under this hood. Could I be allowed to breathe for a bit?'

The man reached forward and lifted the hood up over the nose of Ali Ralston but he didn't let her see anything.

'Breathe in,' said the man. 'As much as you can. I'll put it back down in a moment.'

She sucked in large gulps of air. When the man put the hood back down, Ali Ralston shook again.

'Where are they? Are you sure they're coming? Do you know they're coming?'

'Easy, Ali,' said the motorbike rider. 'They'll be here. It's a good deal. I have a connection to them; you know that.'

'Yes,' said the man who was leading them. 'He has a connection.'

The connection wasn't stated though, thought Clarissa, but then you wouldn't. Ali Ralston was an outsider; saying there was a connection was enough. But the motorcyclist was a deacon, as the books had said. He was quite high up. He was obviously sent out to gain this item.

A van pulled up suddenly, and as it did so, the back door was opened. Nobody got out. Instead, the hooded figure led first the motorcyclist to the van, helping him gently inside, followed by Ali Ralston.

'Where are we going?' she asked.

'You'll see soon enough. Just watch, you have to climb into this van. We'll then sit you down properly. It's perfectly safe, but we need to do this. You need to trust us,' said the man.

Clarissa was almost laughing inside. 'You need to trust us.' Yet you don't trust her to see your face. When somebody placed a bag over your head to take you somewhere, and didn't let you see who they were, it easily meant they could harm you. Clarissa wouldn't have stood for that. In the arts world, you had to trust the other person and that meant seeing their eyes. That meant judging them. Picking out if they were trying to take you for a ride or not.

She texted Patterson, telling him to get into the car. She then texted Ferguson, saying the van was about to leave, and passing on the registration. Slowly, Clarissa moved away, crossing the road well up the hill from the van. She heard it drive off rather than see it happen, at which point she ran for her little green sports car. Jumping inside, she saw Patterson was already there. She started the car up and drove off.

'Eh, headlights,' said Patterson.

'We're following them. They don't want to see a car come straight after them. When we're back on the main road. I'll get the lights on.'

'Can you see?' asked Patterson suddenly, his hand shooting out in front of him.

'Well enough, I mean my reactions are quite good,' said Clarissa. She watched the second hand come out in front of him. He checked his belt. Clarissa laughed, but she focused hard, too. It wasn't easy driving at night like this. You had to look at the road; you had to be very aware of where everything was.

The van drove out and joined the road heading towards the Boat of Garten. Ferguson messaged she was on its tail and Clarissa put the lights on the little green sports car. There was an audible sigh of relief from Patterson.

'It's fine, Pats. We'll find out where they're going and then we'll observe them from there.'

'As easy as that.'

'As easy as that. We don't want to be getting too close. We've done well tonight, on the trail.' *Got this cracked and we don't need a Rottweiler*, she said to herself. *I don't know what Macleod's on about sometimes.*

Chapter 20

As Clarissa drove along the road, her phone vibrated, showing a call was coming in. She pressed the hands free and heard Sabine Ferguson on the other end of the call.

'They're pulling up. I'm driving on past because they're going up a small road. From the looks of it, there's a large barn further up, about five miles from where we started.'

'I think I'm only about a quarter of a mile behind you,' said Clarissa. 'I'll pull by, and we'll check it out. You stay at a distance, Sabine. You're our backup, okay? I'll go in close. If we get too close and something happens, we'll press the panic buttons, and you can bring everyone in.'

'That's understood. I take it that's just a text message because you don't have a panic button, do you?'

'I'll get a message to you, don't worry,' said Clarissa. As she closed the call, Patterson stared towards her. 'We really could do with something like a panic button.'

'The best panic button you can ever have,' said Clarissa, 'is yourself. You need to look after yourself when you're out here. Anyway, we're just doing surveillance. Keep your eyes peeled for where this barn is.'

A few minutes later, Clarissa drove past a small side road. Looking up towards the end of that track, she saw a barn with doors which were slightly open. There wasn't much light around it. Clarissa thought that there was maybe only candlelight streaming out from inside. She drove on past, then pulled the car up off the road into a nearby driveway. She parked it up because the house was dark.

'You're leaving it here,' said Patterson.

'I don't want to leave it out on the road,' said Clarissa. 'I've got to look after this car. It's mine, and besides, if they're patrolling up and down, we don't want it to be seen. So come on, let's go.'

Patterson couldn't dally because Clarissa was out of the car well ahead of him. She stole out of the house's driveway, back onto the road, quickly jumping a fence and entering the fields. The night was dark, clouds having covered over what moonlight there would have been. She could see about fifteen feet in front of her. Keeping her eyes focused on the rough grass, she crept across the fields before she eventually went down on one knee to be joined by Patterson.

'There's people in—well, they're in, like, cloaks and stuff with hoods,' said Patterson. 'I know they said it was a secret society, but I didn't think it would be like this.'

'If they're arts people, they're going to love the drama of it, aren't they?' whispered Clarissa. 'We need to get in there.'

'Whoa,' said Patterson. 'What do you mean?'

'Exactly what I say,' said Clarissa. 'We need to get in. If we're not inside, we can't see what's going on. They may produce the diamond. We want to see who takes it away?'

'You said nothing about this.'

'I thought they were going to do an exchange on the edge of

Loch Garten. I didn't realise we were going inside a barn.'

'Well, we should get backup first. We should wait here until backup arrives,' said Patterson.

'Pats, no. Okay. I'm the boss. We're going to get inside.'

'How are you planning on doing that?' asked Patterson.

'It's pretty sealed off, isn't it?' said Clarissa. 'Come on, we'll have a bit of a further look. See if there's any way of getting in round the back.'

Clarissa looked over at Patterson before taking off into the dark again. She stayed low as she ran across the grass. Some of the minor hillocks provided some cover from the figures who were outside the barn. It was all very melodramatic, and as she went round to the rear of the barn, she saw more of the figures.

That was the other thing, though, wasn't it? If they kept it looking like a society, nobody would take it seriously. It was all just costume play. They weren't a real society. A real society would have men in suits, women dressed smartly and discuss things properly. They wouldn't enact this sort of thing. It was a cover in itself. *Clever*, thought Clarissa, *brilliant*.

Patterson came up beside her again, whispering in her ear.

'It's no different front and back. There are all those guys. We're not going to just walk in. I mean, what's your plan? What are we going to do? Jump one of this lot, don their outfit and run in?'

Clarissa stayed silent but looked at him.

'No. We can't do that.'

'Why not?' asked Clarissa.

'Because you don't do that in the police. We're not—'

'You're not on the murder team. You're with me. I need to be in there. We're undercover, remember?'

'No, we're not. We're on surveillance.'

'No,' said Clarissa. 'We're about to go undercover. I'm going to get in there. You're going to help me take one of these guys out.'

'What do you mean take him out?'

'I didn't mean going to kill him. We'll just tie him up. Secure him. Maybe knock him out.'

'Have you got anything to tie him up with?' asked Patterson.

'No. Go back to the car and open the boot. You'll find some rope and stuff. And a good gag. Should be able to keep him quiet for a while.'

'Why have you got this stuff in your car?'

'The rope's just in case the car breaks down. You're able to pull a small lorry with my rope.'

'You do know you get those metal bars nowadays. Or you can just call the AA.'

'No, no, no. It's just the old-style ropes you need. Don't worry about it.'

'Well, what's the gag for, then?' asked Patterson.

'Oh, the gag,' said Clarissa. 'Oh, don't worry about that either. You see, I need that. It's for my legs. I'm able to do like a sort of tourniquet in case they get sore.'

Patterson looked at her. 'Never heard of doing that for a sore leg.'

'You haven't got to my age yet,' she said. 'Just get them, okay?'

'I could stay and watch. You could do it.'

'I'm the senior officer and I'm also the senior citizen. I'm not legging it back there. Get them, Pats. Do it now. Here are the keys.'

Clarissa sat watching the building in front of her while Patterson disappeared off. She felt like rain was about to arrive,

167

but it stayed off while a wind blew across, masking any sounds from the building. The wind was cool, but not like a winter wind. It was, after all, early spring.

The people outside didn't rotate, and they didn't talk to each other. They only had their own little space to guard. One of them seemed to roam further than the others. *He is the one to go for*, thought Clarissa. She sat and watched him until Patterson came back.

'Did you get them?'

'Yes,' said Patterson. 'Here's your tow rope, conveniently cut up into several pieces. And look, here's that thing you look after your legs with.'

'Good,' said Clarissa. 'That one over there.'

'What?' said Patterson.

'Pats, that one over there; that's who we're going for. Watch him. He'll walk out quite far here. When he goes beyond this little hillock, that's the time to take him.'

'Take him with what?'

'Don't you worry about that. I'll do that,' she said. 'All you've got to do is follow me.'

Clarissa disappeared off, leaving Patterson sitting there. A minute later, he saw her moving from another direction, waving towards him, and he followed her over. Lying on the ground was an unconscious but breathing man, now devoid of the cloak and hood that he'd been wearing. Clarissa put the item on.

'Pats,' she said. 'You tie him up, secure him, make sure he's well away from the others, and I want you to watch while I'm going in. If it goes wrong, just call. Get Macleod and everybody else here.'

'What?'

168

'Get Macleod and everybody else here.'

Patterson shook his head as he tied up the individual. There was a flurry of clothing before Clarissa turned and looked at Patterson. 'How do I look? Good?'

'You look like somebody who's picked the wrong Halloween costume,' said Patterson. 'It looks big on you.'

'Everything looks big on me,' said Clarissa. 'Just my compact shape.'

Patterson smiled at her, but his eyes said she didn't have a compact shape.

'Anyway, time to get on with it,' said Clarissa. She went to walk off, but Patterson stopped her.

'How are you going to get in? Maybe they've got a code word or something.'

'I don't know, I'll just blag it.'

'Think about it,' said Patterson. 'When I read that book, some had the mark that said deacon, yeah? There were higher up people than that, but deacons were servicing the place, running here and there, doing lots of stuff. Maybe we need to sort you out.'

'What do you mean?' asked Clarissa.

Patterson reached inside his jacket and took out a marker pen. 'Give me a wrist,' he said.

She stuck her arm out and Patterson drew on it the marking that they'd seen on both the bodyguard of Lord Harwich and also on the motorbike rider.

'That's a good job,' said Clarissa. 'I couldn't draw it that well. I won't even say anything to them, but just show them that.'

'The ranks in these organisations, according to the book, are very strict. When you're higher up, you expect to be obeyed. I suppose it's the way any good organisation runs, a bit of fear.'

'That's understood,' said Clarissa. 'Keep a watch on me, yes?'

'By the way,' said Patterson, 'why is he unconscious? What did you do to him?'

'I did not hit him on the head,' said Clarissa.

She walked off. Patterson watched her closely, half shaking his head.

As Clarissa walked round towards the barn, she wondered if Patterson would ever find out about the old wrestling techniques she'd learned back in the day. Get up close, get your arm round him. You can choke them into submission; unconsciousness maybe for a minute or two and then you can tie them up. An element of surprise was required and a good powerful arm.

When she'd seen the man she was going to overcome, Clarissa decided he seemed to be robust, but not strong and a perfect target. Patterson didn't need to know; he just needed to get with it. He certainly wouldn't tell Macleod. They'd only been assisted by the man in getting a disguise.

Clarissa approached the front door and suddenly three of the men in their cloaks and hoods came together to close her path. She approached slowly and held her wrist out, showing the markings that were on them.

'Forgive me,' said one man. He stepped aside and opened a small door. Clarissa ignored all the men, simply walking forward and stepping inside.

Her eyes squinted, for even though it was candlelight, it was bright compared to outer darkness. She could see a hooded man at the front. He was one of twelve, dressed similarly to Clarissa. Standing in the middle of the circle was Ali Ralston, along with the motorcycle man.

Ali looked nervous, scanning all around her at these crazy

people in their outfits. Clarissa could tell that the motorcycle man was nervous also. The man who was speaking looked over towards Clarissa suddenly. She turned, stepped back a few paces, so that she was now up against the wall.

For whatever reason, this seemed to satisfy the man. Happy that she wasn't barging into the situation. Maybe he thought she was a guard. Maybe they checked every once in a while. She wasn't sure, but whatever was happening, she was okay.

Clarissa watched the motorcycle man. His hands were free and one of them was inside a pocket. That's where it was. That's the gem he came to pass on.

Ali Ralston, however, was getting even more nervous. 'Excuse me,' she said. 'Where's our money? Where's the briefcases with the money?'

'We'll get on to that in just a moment,' said the man. 'We need to make sure that you're unaccompanied.'

'Has there been any motion outside? Has anything been seen?' The man was now looking over at Clarissa. She shook her head inside the hood.

'Good,' said the man. 'Remain here, at the door, until the transition.'

Clarissa tried to show that she was an imposing figure by the door, but her stature fostered little hope of looking like a squat sentry. It didn't seem to matter though, as the man leading the circle lifted his hands up and started speaking in a language she didn't understand. Do you speak Sanskrit? she wondered. Was it just written? Was this Sanskrit? Or was it something else?

A chanting began, and some of the circle chanted as well, on and on and on in a wild frenzy. And then suddenly, it stopped. Ali Ralston was shaking, spinning round, looking at the different figures. The motorcycle man put his hand out, grabbing hers.

'It's perfectly normal,' he said to her, but Clarissa could tell he was nervous, too.

Then the hooded man at the front said, 'Now is the time. It's ahead of us. It's here for us. It's time to make the exchange.'

Chapter 21

'Forgive me, Miss Ralston, you'll have to be covered with the hood again. Unfortunately, I need to examine the item to make sure it's exactly what you say it is and I can't do that with this hood on.'

The man who spoke was clearly the leader, but from either side a figure approached, dressed in cloak and hood, and placed a black hood back over Ali Ralston. However, the motorcycle man remained uncovered. That made sense to Clarissa, especially if he was part of their group. He would know who they were. They would understand he was a deacon after all. Surely, he would have known nearly everyone in this group.

Ali Ralston was a truckload of nerves as she stood there, unable to see what was going on. Clarissa didn't move, watching from within her disguise as the man in charge gave an approving nod to his two colleagues, who had covered Ali's head.

'Gillan,' said the man at the front. 'It's time to hand it over. Everyone, the Esoteric Tear is here, within our grasp at last. The chance of a lifetime. The chance to be prepared finally for the end times. Something of such power is not to be treated lightly. And we should be thankful that we have it.'

He spoke again, in a tongue that Clarissa didn't recognise. Then he put his hand out, clearly expecting that Gillan, the motorcycle man, would hand it over. Gillan took the gem out of his pocket and pressed it forward into the leader's palm. It reflected some of the candlelight.

Clarissa thought it wasn't an unattractive gem, but it wasn't worth all this nonsense. The leader picked up the gem and studied it. He slowly bent over and Gillan stepped closer until he was looking up and into the face of the man. Previously, it must have been hidden by the hood, but now, Gillan could see who was talking. And Gillan erupted.

'It's not Fallon! It's not Fallon! Ali, get out! Get out!'

There was a moment of shock. It was like the world suddenly froze while everyone digested what had just been shouted. Clarissa, almost involuntarily, migrated without thinking towards the ring of people. She wasn't sure what she was going to do as the diamond was whisked away into the pocket of the leader.

Gillan stepped forward to grab him, but from behind, one of the hooded men seized Gillan. A knife suddenly flashed in the candlelight and Clarissa sprinted forward. She saw the knife being whipped across Gillan's throat, blood spattering out.

She'd been there on surveillance, been there to watch people. Was there an innocent party here? Her reactions took over, and she went to the one she thought was most innocent. Ali had a hood on. They'd just killed Gillan. The leader had the gem. She'd be next, surely. She'd be the one they'd go for.

Clarissa hit one man in the circle from behind with her shoulder, sending him spinning. She then reached over and grabbed Ali, pulling her back as a knife was slashed at her.

Clarissa's other hand came up and whipped off the hood, pulling Ali behind her. The man with the knife, who had slit Gillan's throat, stepped towards Clarissa. He was going to lunge.

A clean fighter would have maybe stepped to one side, grabbed his wrist, pushed him past them. But Clarissa wasn't a clean fighter. Clarissa needed every advantage she should get. She spun and grabbed one of the man's colleagues, pulling him by the arm, twisting with every ounce of strength she had. She spun the man straight into the knife that was being thrust out towards her. There followed a cry of pain, but Clarissa turned to see Ali.

She was going to grab her and run, but Ali was already underway, taking off, clattering into someone, and then trying to scrabble to her feet. Clarissa ran to protect her, as the man with the knife was in pursuit.

Some candles were on holders, almost a person high, and Clarissa grabbed one of these, swinging it behind her, catching the man with the knife on the shoulder. It connected, knocked him off balance, but didn't put him to the ground. So, Clarissa hit him again, and again.

Another man then stepped in to intervene in his hood and cloak, but Clarissa jabbed him with the candleholder. The flame had gone out, but he got hit squat in the belly with the hot wax that was still inside the candle. He yelled, and Clarissa turned to see the knife being pushed towards her again. She hit the hand that held it with the candle holder, but the angle was awkward, causing her to twist and the candle holder fell out of her hands. The knife, however, had been pushed to one side and so she ran.

She looked over towards the door and saw Ali opening it

and running, but then someone stepped across, blocking the exit. Clarissa went to run towards the door but another man was standing there. She'd never get through two of them and with the man with the knife still after her, she needed to keep on the move.

Clarissa grabbed the man closest to her, pulling at his cloak, hauling it down one arm. It came away off that arm, spinning him round so that he impeded the man with the knife. The other arm still had the garment attached to it, but Clarissa pulled hard, causing the man to topple over.

She pulled the garment towards her, wrapping it tight as she saw the man with the knife coming. He stabbed at her, and she put the garment in front of her and the knife sailed into it. She wrapped it round his hand quickly as he threw a punch towards her. It caught her on the shoulder and she cried out, but she held on, keeping the garment around the knife.

He reached for her, putting a hand up, and began to choke her. Her heart pounded. He had her held tight. She was in trouble.

Clarissa swung her hand up towards his face and her fingernails clawed into him. So desperate was she, needing to be quick for fear others around may jump her too, she dug her nails as deep as she could. They drew blood and she saw it drip down the man's face.

But he didn't release her, not until she got close to his eye. She jabbed a finger into the eyeball. He shouted, his hand coming off her throat, and she pushed him back. Letting go of the cloak which was still wrapped around the knife in his hand, she turned and ran only to be grabbed by the leader.

He pulled her close, and Clarissa drove her head upwards, catching the man under his chin. She heard his teeth clatter and pushed him back again. But she had nowhere to run. She had to get out of here. There were too many of them running around. How would she ever get out?

Someone grabbed her arms, holding her tight, and the hood fell down off the man who was in charge. He looked over at a compatriot who had been fighting Clarissa with the knife.

'Give me that. I'll sort this one. I'll get her to talk as well.'

He took the knife and began marching towards Clarissa. 'First, we'll give her a puncture wound, then she'll die slowly if she doesn't get help. And if she doesn't talk quick enough, we won't throw her out on the road. She can just bleed to death in here.'

There was a laugh from the leader until one of them asked about Ali Ralston.

'She doesn't matter. We've got it. She doesn't know who we are. She doesn't know why we're here. There'll be nothing in this barn in half an hour's time. Forget her. If you see her, finish her. But for the moment, let's just forget her.'

He turned, knife in hand, and marched towards Clarissa. 'We'll just drive it into your belly. Make you bleed.'

Clarissa's feet scrabbled for purchase, trying to push away. But the man got closer and closer. Another man joined him on his right-hand side. He indicated to the leader that he could do the job for him.

'I'll do this, brother. Don't worry,' said the leader. 'I'm skilled in what they call the subtle art of persuasion. It won't be a problem. She'll break, and she'll break quickly.'

The man in the cloak and hood beside him looked briefly towards the leader, but without revealing much of his face. When he looked back towards Clarissa, more seemed on show. Clarissa thought the nose seemed very familiar.

The man drew back the knife and Clarissa squirmed, but her hands were held fast by others. She tried to brace herself for the pain that was about to come.

The cloaked man beside the leader suddenly turned away from her. She didn't see him as he picked something up. The next thing she knew, he was battering the knife wielding leader. The knife fell from the man's hands, and he tumbled to the floor.

Clarissa stood in shock until the piece of wood the man had been using was thrust past her head, missing it by a few inches. It clattered into the person holding her and he tumbled backwards. The man in the hood took a hold of her and started pulling her towards the door.

Several people closed ranks and the hooded man stopped, grabbing one, stepping past him and drilling him to the floor. Clarissa gave a hard kick in the shins to one man standing nearby. She then followed up by grabbing his throat and pushing him backwards. As he stumbled, his head hit the wall, and he fell to the ground. The man who was helping her took another person out of the way and pulled open the door of the barn.

'Go,' shouted Clarissa, but the man shook his head, showing she should run. Clarissa stepped outside and threw herself backwards as something swung towards her. It looked like a large piece of wood or club. And then she looked up into the face of a man in a hood standing over her.

He raised the club up, about to bring it down on top of her, when he was suddenly tackled by someone running out from inside the building. There was a scuffle, but Clarissa didn't wait for the outcome, getting back up on her feet. She saw two hooded men fight, one raining punches down into the face of the other as he got on top of him. It was over so quickly. Clarissa reached down to help the winner up. She thought it was the man who had fought for her inside, and she grabbed his hand, dragging him off across the fields.

She was wearing the green shawl underneath, and she was as hot as anything, through all the exertion and tension she'd just been through. There were shouts from people behind her, but she kept running, the man who had helped her, right on her heels. It took them a few minutes to get round to where the car was parked.

Clarissa shouted at him to get in, telling him not to worry. It was her car. She sat down and went to turn the ignition. There were no keys in her pocket. *Damn it, Patterson had them. Where the hell was Patterson?*

The man in the cloak and hood had jumped into the car beside her. He pulled his hood down and reached over with the keys. Patterson was looking straight at her.

'You looking for these?' he said.

Chapter 22

Clarissa wanted to reach forward and kiss him. But she took the keys and turned on the engine, flooring it out of the driveway, out onto the road. She went the opposite direction from the way she came in, looking to put as much distance as possible.

'Do we call backup in? Round them up?'

'No,' said Clarissa, 'we don't. We need to find Ali Ralston.'

'What happened to her?'

'Weren't you in there?' asked Clarissa.

'Only when it all kicked off, the door opened. I subdued one guy outside and came in wearing the outfit.'

'Ali Ralston got out. I saved her and she got out. I don't know where she went.'

'And?' asked Patterson.

'And something went wrong. The motorbike guy, his name was Gillan. He saw the guy who was leading in there. And it wasn't Fallon, whoever the hell Fallon is. We need to get Ali Ralston. We need to find out what's going on. The diamond's on the move. Or it will be.'

'We could stop it,' said Patterson. 'We call in now.'

'It won't work,' said Clarissa. 'There'll be away with it. Yeah, we'll find the odd person who will not be very helpful. But the people at the top, they'll be out of there by now.'

'So, what do we do?'

'We find Ferguson and we get on top of this. And we find Ali Ralston.'

Clarissa's heart was pounding now. She had come through it. She was alive, but her problems were only just increasing. Of course she should phone Macleod, but dammit, she didn't want to talk to him. Instead, she reached underneath, found her phone, and called Sabine.

'Sabine, join up with us. We've got to find Ali Ralston. It's all gone to pot. Somebody's away with the Tear.'

'Got you,' said Sabine. Clarissa was amazed at the calmness of the woman, despite all that was going on. 'I think I see you whizzing past me just now. Do we double tail back? How do we do this?'

Clarissa slammed the brakes, stopping in the middle of the road. 'Put the phone down and come and talk to me,' she said. 'And let's get somebody to go back in and have a look at that place. Uniform, though. No special deal. Just uniform.' Clarissa watched Ferguson pull up in the car, jump out of it and run over to the little green sports car.

'So, what's the plan?'

'We need to fan out. She can't have gone far from here. She doesn't even know where she is.'

'No,' said Ferguson. 'But, to be honest, she'll soon find out—wouldn't you? I mean, we're near Boat of Garten. She's a local girl, isn't she?'

Both of them looked at Patterson.

'Am I the only one that does the research?'

'Just tell me,' barked Clarissa.

'She was born up this way. She worked for Scottish Museums down in the Edinburgh and Glasgow region. But she has her house up here. Everything's up here. She'll know the place as soon as she can identify somewhere.'

'Great. She might even have friends,' said Clarissa. 'Right. Start sweeping the roads. Out and about. I'll have to talk to the boss.'

'Good luck with that one,' said Sabine.

'Should we have played it any different?' asked Clarissa.

'I backed you,' said Sabine. 'I'll take the flack with you.'

'I'm the boss. I'll take that,' said Clarissa. 'But do me a favour. Find her. Find her quick.'

'You better take the car and drive,' she said to Patterson.

'No,' said Patterson. 'You drive. I'll look. You can talk while driving. I'll be on the lookout. You can't drive and look at the same time.'

He's right about me being on the phone, thought Clarissa. *But look and drive at the same time? Of course I can.*

She was angry at herself, angry at the situation, angry that things had gone wrong. This was her leading the Arts team. This was meant to go right, meant to be the pièce de résistance. She was going to come out victorious. Macleod would know he could just let her get on with it. The same way he just let Hope get on with things.

Clarissa started the car up, heading off in the opposite direction. A call came in on her phone. This would be Ferguson with some questions. She took the call on the hands-free set, waiting for a pickup.

'Macleod, what's going on?'

'What do you mean?'

'I mean, what's going on? You'd have headed back here,

wanted to show me the triumph you had.'

'We found them, okay, in Loch Garten. They got into a van. The van then went to this barn, just outside of the Boat of Garten. We got inside where they were going to make a handover, except it looks like they weren't the right people for them to deal with.'

'So, where's the Esoteric Tear?'

'The Tear is currently in the hands of whoever the other people were.'

'And we don't know who they are,' said Macleod.

'No. I do know who the biker was, though. A man by the name of Gillan.'

'Well, that's a positive,' said Macleod.

'It's not. He's dead.'

'What? Explain,' said Macleod.

'When they went inside and they went to hand it over, Gillan must have realised that they weren't the right people. I think it's the other faction. They'd lured them in to hand it over.'

'So, what you're telling me,' said Macleod, 'is one faction's nicked it from the others who had paid to get it robbed for them, and they're going to go after them. They're going to—'

'Don't. I've also got Ali Ralston out on the loose. I've got Ferguson and myself looking for them. But we need to get people in. We need to get forensics all over this barn. We need to—'

'And I need to get somebody here to look after this woman that I'm babysitting.'

'Look, sorry, Seoras, it didn't go—'

'Don't, we need to deal with the now. Get on the lookout; find Ali Ralston, okay? I'll get forensic and people into that barn. Were you able to pick up anybody else coming out of it?'

'We fled. They tried to knife me.'

'Are you okay?'

'Thanks to Patterson. Patterson came in and got me out.'

'Well,' said Macleod, 'that's good.' His tone was quiet, though. He didn't sound ecstatic.

'I'll get on the hunt. I'll speak to you soon,' said Clarissa.

In the dark, it was hard enough seeing anything. You had to look away from your own headlights, and in that, Patterson had been correct. Clarissa was driving, trying to watch the road. When she looked into the darkness, her eyes couldn't adjust quick enough. Patterson, however, kept his eyes shielded from the headlights.

They drove for two hours, round and round the Boat of Garden area, eventually making their way out further.

'She could be anywhere by now,' said Clarissa. A call came through from Sabine Ferguson.

'Somebody making it back late from a party and I mean properly late, saw a woman get on a bus about an hour ago. She could be anywhere. She matched the description of Ralston.'

'Bugger!' said Clarissa. 'Bugger, Bugger! Right, route back to the barn. Okay. We will not find her like this. We've done what we can. If you can come up with any ideas on the way, Sabine, it'll be appreciated.'

Clarissa turned the car around driving back to the location of the barn. As she arrived, she saw the police cars outside, and a forensic wagon had turned up. Clarissa parked up on the edge of the cordon showing her warrant card to the constable on duty. She found Jona Nakamura on scene.

'He's dead inside, isn't he?' she asked Jona upon seeing her.

'There's one dead. There's nobody else about. Knife wound. Pretty brutal. Throat.'

'Yeah,' said Clarissa. 'Throat wounds seemed to be following me around at the moment. Couldn't save this one.'

She went to storm off, but Jona caught her arm. 'Whoa!' she said. 'Ease up.'

'Don't!' raged Clarissa. 'He's coming here now. He's going to want an explanation. It's all gone to rat. Don't give me ease up. I need to—well, I need to—'

'You need to stop,' said Jona.

Clarissa shook her head, but Jona put a hand on each shoulder. 'Look at me, Clarissa; look at me!' Clarissa looked away.

'Urquhart!' Clarissa felt a slap on her face. Shocked, she turned and glowered at Jona.

'Good, you're listening now. Get your head into this, okay? You've taken a hit. It's rubbish, it's all going down the spout, fine, but you will not get anywhere by running around like this. Think. It's time to stop, it's time to engage the brain, and it's time to think. Okay?'

'Okay,' said Clarissa.

Patterson came up behind her, but Jona put a hand up to him. 'Give us a moment, okay? Talk to Jackson there. He'll fill you in on what's going on.'

'Okay, Eric,' said Clarissa.

Eric sauntered off, and Jona turned her attention back to Clarissa. 'It goes wrong for everyone, every now and again. When it goes wrong for Macleod, what does he do? He stops. He focuses. Hope, she stops; she focuses. Hope slows down. She's learnt that from him.

'You've charged in. You've done it the way you think you should do it, and it hasn't worked. That's fine. Now you've got to find out a way to make it work. I'll look in here, dig up what evidence I can. I'll see if I can attach anything to the persons in the case. But, to be honest, I don't know if you're going to find anything with the forensics in here. We'll see. You know what it's like with forensics. You can get lucky. But it usually backs up other evidence rather than provides the conclusive piece.'

'I know,' said Clarissa. 'I was just hoping.'

'You were just hoping I could make it all go magically away. I'm a forensic investigator, not your fairy godmother. I was never quite tall enough for that.'

'Fairy godmothers are small.'

'The one in Cinderella wasn't,' said Jona.

'Sure, she was.'

'Not from dizzying heights.'

For a moment, the women stopped, looking at each other, and Clarissa cracked a smile.

'What's next?' Clarissa asked.

Jona looked over her shoulder. 'Well, I think he's next,' she said.

Clarissa spun round and saw a car arriving that she recognised. The door opened and out stepped Macleod, wearing a long coat over a suit and tie. She swore that the constable standing next to him almost jumped on seeing him. Seoras didn't look happy.

'I don't think he's that bad actually at the moment,' said Jona, apparently reading Clarissa's mind. 'I've seen him worse.'

'No, you haven't.'

'The door's still on the hinge of the car. I reckon he'd have taken it off if he'd been really annoyed.'

'Here goes,' she said.

'You're his Rottweiler,' said Jona. 'Stand your ground and

show some teeth.'

Clarissa looked at the small woman for a moment and then gave a nod. She was right. This wasn't the time for Clarissa to go into her shell. She strode over towards Macleod but he was heading straight for the barn.

'You're going to want to put a coverall on, if you're going to go in there.'

'Well, good evening, Detective Inspector,' said Macleod. 'I just thought I'd see the scene before I talked to you.'

'It went wrong, all right? Badly wrong. It was going to go wrong whether or not I was inside there.'

'Well, we could have been on the outside. We could have swooped. We could have—'

'And what would we have? The diamond and nothing else up above and they would just keep coming for it. I keep telling you this. I keep trying to get this into your thick skull.'

Maybe she'd just gone overboard because he turned with a face that she'd never seen on Macleod before.

'Over there, now,' he said. Macleod marched Clarissa over to a patch of ground where no one was standing. They were maybe a good hundred metres from the nearest police personnel.

'One, you don't speak to me like that. Okay? Two, never, ever, ever speak to me like that,' said Macleod. 'Three. I'm the boss, for a reason. Four. I let you do what you thought was best. I wasn't entirely in agreement, but I let you do it. Therefore, all this that's going on, is my fault. It's on me. It's not just on you, it's on me. And I'm mighty cheesed off about it too. Five. I've got another dead person. I've got people back at the station saying, everywhere Macleod goes, it's murder, whatever team he's on. Okay? I've got a woman who's scared out of her wits back at a safe house because more bodies are going down, wondering, can we ever end this?'

'But that's what we're trying to do,' said Clarissa. 'I'm trying to end it.'

Macleod stared off into the distance. 'Can we? How does this end? Tell me. Tell me what the scene was inside there.'

'They're like a society. They were all in cloaks and hoods. Secret society.'

'Like the Templars, you said. You sit and you tell me I don't know about the art. I listen and take it in. In my head I have a perfect picture of what's going on. And these guys, these guys won't stop until that stone is either disintegrated or so far away from them, they can never hope to get it back.'

'Don't you think I know that?' said Clarissa. 'That's why I was—'

'You've done what you've done. It went wrong. Gillan wasn't clever enough to realise he was being double crossed. Ali Ralston is alive. We need to find her. She could be dead soon. From what you've said, she's not part of the group. Therefore, either side is likely to torture her to find out where it is. If Gillan was the contact, if Gillan was the man who went to his side of the society—well, they'll all think that she knows something about it. So, they'll hunt her, whether to get the stone back or not.'

'I get that. You know? I get that,' said Clarissa. 'We'll put a search out for her. We've got the station looking for her.' Macleod went to turn away. Clarissa tapped him on the shoulder. 'Don't,' she said. 'Don't. I need you now. I need you. Because we need to know where to go. We need to work it out.'

'You're the DI,' said Macleod. 'You don't need me. I'm the

DCI above this. It's your investigation. I'm letting you run it. You don't need me. You just need to tell me what you're doing. Stop looking to me. Solve it. Work it out.'

Clarissa went silent for a moment. Macleod turned away. The hardest bit of seeing him was the fact he looked disappointed in her. She could just chuck all this. She could get home to Frank. Get home and away from this. She didn't need to be here. She could retire. Frank had money. She had money. They could have been happily retired.

But she came back to this. Why the hell did she come back to this? Her head went down. She fought back a few tears and then it hit her.

The van. Where the hell's the van? They brought the pair of them here in the van. They must think somebody had clocked the van. If somebody was here, if somebody tailed Gillan, if somebody tried to rescue him, if somebody got Ali out, they'd have thought the the van. They'd have been followed in the van. They'll be getting rid of the van.

She lifted her head. 'Seoras! The van. They came here in a van. They think I rescued her. The van. They think the van's been tailed. They'll be getting rid of the van.'

'Very good,' he said. 'Go get it.' Calmly, he turned and walked off towards the scene of the crime again. She could have hated him for that. There was no-well-done, there was no-that's-it rallying cry. In fact, he almost ignored her, telling her to get on with it. She could feel the adrenaline picking up. She'd show him; she'd damn well show him.

'Patterson!' she shouted. 'Ferguson, on me.'

Chapter 23

Ferguson, Patterson and Clarissa were in the little green sports car.

'The van was here,' said Clarissa. 'They brought them in the van. They'll think that we've seen the van. He even helped them out of it at the barn. Therefore, they'll be getting rid of the van. I think they'll burn it. Don't take a risk hiding it. If you hide it, and it's found, we know where they are. They'll just burn it out, just get rid of it.'

'And you think they're doing that now?' asked Patterson.

'She's right,' said Sabine. 'I would. I'd get rid of it as soon as possible. I wouldn't risk it for a moment. Somebody's dead in that barn; police are all over it. They're going to be thinking that the police could start putting pressure on. If it's two factions, people could let names slip out. They're going to know who's in the factions. After all, there was a split.'

'Exactly,' said Clarissa. 'So, we need to find a van on fire somewhere. You're going to burn it, aren't you? That's the easiest thing to do. Set it on fire. Just get rid of it.'

'It's been a couple of hours, though. Might even have burnt through by now, surely,' said Ferguson.

'Let's hit the road. Get your car,' she said to Ferguson. 'And let's get out there. See if we can see anything.'

'We saw nothing before,' said Ferguson. 'We scoured here for a couple of hours, looking for Ali Ralston. And we didn't see any fires then.'

'Drive down paths off the main road. You could burn it away from—' Sabine almost tutted. 'What's your point,' asked Clarissa, 'or are you just making noise?'

'The point is, we need to be up there,' said Sabine, pointing to the sky. 'Call in for a police helicopter.'

'It'll be coming up from Glasgow then, won't it?' said Clarissa. 'Okay, so we'll have to wait a bit, but—'

Overhead was the sound of a helicopter passing over, which paused Clarissa in the middle of her speech.

'What's that?' she asked.

Patterson looked up. 'Coastguard? Coastguard probably coming back from a job.'

'Why are you saying that?' asked Clarissa.

'Heading towards Inverness. That's where the base is. Or one of the bases. This time of night they rarely fly around routinely. I mean, it's nearly six in the morning.'

'So, we need to get a hold of them. We need to get a number then.'

'I'll get you a number,' said Patterson. 'Local station's in Stornoway. I'll call it.'

Patterson picked up his phone and a moment later was talking to an operative on the other end of the line.

'They're trying to get contact. They've got to go through their aeronautical side or something. I said you'd give the authority for it.'

'The authority for it. Just tell them!' said Clarissa. She grabbed the phone. 'Hello, who am I speaking to?'

'This is Tim. I'm the senior officer on tonight,' he said. 'It's not normal to do this, but I've contacted our aeronautical section. We're just waiting for the go ahead from them. They talk to the helicopters. We're not allowed to just task them wherever we want.'

'My name is Detective Inspector Clarissa Urquhart. I'm in the pursuit of a crime, I would like your assistance. Make sure they're aware of that, please.'

'Absolutely, just a moment.'

Clarissa held on to the phone. She looked up and saw that the helicopter was now circling. Tim came back a moment later.

'They're talking to the helicopter. They want to know what you need. I believe he's circling at the moment.'

'I can actually see him,' said Clarissa. 'You can probably hear him in the background. Tim, I want them to look for any fires. Any minor source of heat. Whatever. We believe we've had a van burnt out somewhere near our current location. Have they got something that can look for heat?'

'I think so,' said Tim. 'They usually have some sort of infrared camera. I'll talk to them, see what they can do.'

Clarissa waited on the end of the phone.

'They're on the move,' said Patterson.

Clarissa looked up and saw the helicopter no longer flying in a circle. They were starting to follow a route. Tim came back on the phone.

'Have they found something, Tim?'

'No, they're starting to search. They'll call it in to me. If you give me your number, I'll call you as soon as I've got anything. Or I can get you to talk to them.'

'What, like on a phone?'

'I'm talking to them on the radio. I can patch you through, if need be.'

'Okay, Tim,' said Clarissa. 'You call me as soon as you've got something.'

It was fifteen minutes later when Tim called Clarissa back. Fifteen minutes where she was praying and hoping that something would come up. The case didn't quite depend on it completely, but she needed to get moving. She needed to get a result here.

'This is Tim. They found a source of heat. How close do you want them to go to it? They're a little distance away at the moment. They could go closer and look.'

'Can they film it at all from a distance? I'd rather they didn't sit over the top of it. They could scare someone away.'

'They could put a searchlight on it.'

'No, Tim. Tell them to keep away from it but get as good a picture of it if they can.'

'They're saying it's a significant heat source. It's in a wood,' said Tim. 'They're telling me it's at the end of a small track, something you could drive a van down.'

'Give me the location,' said Clarissa. Tim advised her of where it was exactly.

'We'll check it out,' said Clarissa. 'Ask the pilot to look elsewhere, to continue the search for a bit, in case there are any other places. Make a note of them. Call me if they get anything else, and thank them for their efforts so far.'

Clarissa turned and smiled at her two colleagues. 'Here is where we're going. Sabine, off we go. Follow me.'

The little green car raced along the road before coming to a small track. Patterson was following the map on his phone and said that this was the track that would lead down to the end.

'Well, he can't come back out this way. He can't get picked up. If somebody's still there, we have them.'

'If somebody's still there,' said Patterson. Clarissa pulled off the road and dropped the lights. She slowed the car for a moment. Her eyes would need to become adjusted to being in the dark again. She noticed Patterson's hands going forward, towards the dash.

'Are you sure about this? It's a bit of a risk.'

'If he doesn't see us coming, all the better,' said Clarissa. 'How far are we away?'

'Half a mile.'

Clarissa continued to drive and noted that behind her Sabine had cut her lights as well. A few hundred metres from where the road would finish, Clarissa stopped her car. She turned off the engine and waited for Sabine to do the same before pulling her colleagues towards her.

'We creep up along the road. If we see something, we'll fan out.'

Slowly, the three of them crept up, along the stone-covered path. Clarissa tried to walk quietly. In the distance, she could see a small orange glow. There was a fire, but it was small. As they got closer, Clarissa could see that a van, or rather the remains of a van, were there. It had been heavily burnt out, the smell almost choking. The smoke was drifting towards them.

She crouched down, joined by the others, and tried to scan off ahead.

'Do you think there's anyone there?' she said. Patterson looked closely, but it was Sabine who spotted someone.

'Off behind it to the left, maybe about fifteen metres away.

Someone by that tree.'

'Are you sure?' asked Clarissa, unable to see them.

'Completely,' she said.

'I'll approach from the front. Go towards him. You two circle round. We'll get him in a pincer. You to the right, Pats. Sabine to the left. Be careful. We don't know if he's armed. We don't know who he is. Don't put yourselves at too much risk.'

'We're creeping up on somebody we don't know is armed, or indeed if he's a decent fighter, out of the dark. And you're asking us not to put ourselves at risk. If we don't want to put ourselves at risk,' said Sabine, 'we should stay here.'

'And he'll be gone by the time we get enough backup,' said Clarissa. 'We need that man. If we get that man, we get a link into the other side of the organisation. We get a link into whoever's been silencing people.'

Clarissa sent her colleagues out and thirty seconds later walked quietly towards where the van was burning. As she approached it, she tried to keep an eye out where Sabine had said the man was. But he wasn't there. At least not in as much as she could see. Now that. she was close, the air was choking, smoke still pouring off the van.

Clarissa could smell the rubber that had burnt. There was a cloy taste to the air, and dark thick smoke. However, everything was quiet apart from the odd crack, the odd piece of metal or possibly the door reacting to the extreme heat it had suffered. Warping as it cooled.

She walked around the edge of the vehicle. Then turned and looked at where the man should be. She heard him get up and go, but she didn't see him.

'Got him,' said Sabine. 'He's on the move. Keep going towards the point he was at before.'

'Good job,' said Patterson. Clarissa hoped they could get him in a pincer, hoped they could pull him in. Ferguson was out wide. She had her torch out now, shining it into the distance. Clarissa didn't have one with her, but Patterson had his. She followed where their lights were, occasionally seeing a leg or an arm of a man, and then there was a gunshot. The lights dropped.

'Cover,' shouted Clarissa. 'Everyone okay?'

'Fine, fine,' came two cries.

'Keep the lights on him but keep a distance. Keep yourselves in cover.'

Another shot rang out. Clarissa decided that she now would not speak. It would give her position away. The lights were searching in a particular spot, maybe some fifty metres up ahead of her. She stole through the undergrowth quietly, eyes scanning, wishing she had the eyes she had when she was eighteen.

She could see plenty then. Nowadays, things just didn't focus the same, never quite right. She saw a blur by her leg. Carefully, she crept around a tree, creeping her way across the uneven ground below her. She was within ten metres of the man now. He was crouched and had his arms out in front of him, a weapon in his hand. As Clarissa got close to him, she looked ahead to see torchlight swinging around. The man was aiming straight into that position.

Clarissa reached forward, grabbing the wrists of the man, pushing them down as the shot rang out. The bullet had been driven straight into the ground, but Clarissa had her hands on the man's wrists, fighting to keep the gun from going upwards. This was it. This was purely a life and death moment. She'd either hold him, subduing him, or he'd shoot someone.

Clarissa held his hands, pushing them upwards. The man kicked at her knee. She yelped in pain, but her hands hung on. Her knee lifted, she was on one foot, and the man, with the gun still in one hand, tried to free another hand. He couldn't, so he head-butted her.

She reeled, groggy, but she focused on keeping her hands on him, again and again. She felt him slip as he drove a knee up towards her stomach. Her hands came off. She fell towards the ground, half expecting a shot in her direction, thinking it was the end. Something hit the man from the side. He tumbled to the ground. Someone was on top of him, hitting him. Someone else was shouting. They had the firearm. There were a couple of minutes, during which there was noise, then a quiet. Then somebody helped her to sit up.

'We got him, Clarissa,' said Sabine. 'We got him. He's handcuffed, but we're ready to take him back. Are you okay?'

Clarissa half stood up. She looked over at the man in his handcuffs. *They got him. Thank goodness they got him.* She wanted to walk over and kick him. Wanted to drive her heels deep into his neck. She wanted to smack him across the face. He had hit her hard. She'd feel that punch to the stomach for weeks, she was sure of it. And the headbutt. Oh, her head rang.

'Can you see who he is?' asked Sabine.

Clarissa looked. She did not know who that was. Did she? Or was she just . . .

'That's the bodyguard of Lord Harwich,' said Sabine. 'I was there. Still got the mark on his wrist.'

'Call Macleod,' said Clarissa. 'Call Macleod and tell him who we've got. We'll need to move. Harwich has got to be involved in this. He's a collector. He's—'

'Maybe you want to call?'

'No,' said Clarissa. 'I'm not his pet dog. I don't perform tricks and then show them back to him.'

No, she thought. *I'm the Rottweiler.* He riled me up and let me off the leash. She could see it now. She could see Macleod, the way he'd fired her up by antagonising her. *You swine, Seoras,* she thought. *You little swine!*

Chapter 24

Macleod had arranged to meet Clarissa outside the estate of Lord Harwich. There was a squad of uniformed officers on the way who would search the premises. Clarissa had a hunch the man would be involved. He was used to handling artifacts of this type. Anything valuable, he'd have somewhere to keep it. It would be there. She knew it.

Ferguson was going to accompany them, but Patterson had been sent back to the safe house. Lynn Green wasn't out of the woods yet, and Macleod, having previously left her in the company of his partner Jane, wanted Jane replaced as quickly as he could.

Clarissa had wondered at Macleod leaving Jane, but she was the only other one who had known. Macleod really must have worried for the safety of the woman, because to put Jane in such a position was not like him. He clearly didn't trust his police force. Clarissa had found that quite something. He had listened to her; he had listened to what she was saying, how deep these people could reach. For all that he had a go at her, for all that he chastised her, he did believe what she said.

Things were different. Things were so very different now

that she was the DI with no Hope in between. She wondered; did Hope get a lot of this from Macleod? He said nothing to Patterson, nor to Ferguson. He let them do. That was Clarissa's job. Instead, he had gone straight to sort out Clarissa. Maybe that's why Hope looked so annoyed around him these days. Was he doing the same with her?

Lord Harwich did not take kindly to being woken up at seven o'clock in the morning. He'd had a particularly late night the previous evening, apparently. He'd been out drinking. Clarissa wondered had he been there, watching as Gillan died. Had even been one of the people who had attacked her.

The estate house was searched from top to bottom. Clarissa was amazed at how easily the man let them do it. She stood with Macleod as all around her people were searching, Ferguson directing the teams.

'It's not here,' Clarissa said to Macleod.

'You said it would be here. We spoke,' said Macleod, 'and you told me it would be here. He would be the one to have it, was the one with the background in the arts. He was the one who had precious items that could be kept safe.'

'It's not here,' she repeated. 'Not here.'

Ferguson was identifying many of the items that were in Lord Harwich's house. He had a small fortune. But one particular room was the one to hold his pride and joy. Clarissa went through several of the items with Ferguson.

'You find anything,' said Seoras.

'That painting on the far left there,' said Clarissa, 'that's technically stolen. It's small fry; it's not worth talking about. He could blur over that. Say he picked it up from a dealer. Not a problem for him to get away with it. There's no point going into hassle like that.'

'Well, I think there is,' said Macleod. 'What else have you got?'

'That item over there was missing, recently recovered, and has ended up here. The painting up at the back of the room—that's a fake; he doesn't know it.'

'It's a fake?' queried Macleod.

'Oh yeah, that's a fake,' said Clarissa. 'Hard to tell, but that's really my given subject.'

'So, in terms of being a collector, how would you rate him?'

'I'll find out for you.' Clarissa walked over to Lord Harwich. 'Quite a collection.'

'It is. Clarissa Urquhart. I have to say, it's been a disappointment meeting you. I thought you would be better than this.'

'In what way?'

'Well, you're just letting these people sail in, run around. These items are valuable.'

'That painting on the far side is. That's fifty grands' worth. I'd probably put better protection on it than that. The one beside it, ten grand. Not that exciting, but, you know, delightful piece. I actually like the picture,' said Clarissa. 'Statue down the front, forty-five thousand,' she said. Harwich nodded. 'Painting up behind it. Fiver.'

Harwich looked at her. 'So, you really don't know your stuff,' he said. 'That's worth three hundred grand. That was quite hard to get hold of.'

'That's a fake,' said Clarissa. 'Come with me.'

She took him up to it and pointed out the style; she explained how certain strokes were laid on the canvas. Clarissa quoted the history of the painting, explaining that the bottom left-hand corner did not tally in with it. And the signature just wasn't right.

'You're having me on,' he said. 'I see what you're doing. You're trying to unsettle me.'

'Nope,' she said. 'I just know my stuff. Watch. Sabine, what would you value this painting at?' Sabine came over. 'I'm no expert, but what, two to three thousand? Something like that?'

'Absolutely. Fortunately, it's a fake.'

'No,' said Sabine. 'Is it?'

Clarissa took her through the history. Sabine shook her head. Then she picked up her phone and called someone. A couple of minutes later, she put the phone away. 'Sorry to doubt you, boss, but you're right. That is a fake. Are there any more fakes in here?'

'Are you aware if you've got any more fakes?' Clarissa asked Harwich.

'I thought everything in here was genuine.'

'Now there's at least two other fakes, but I will not tell you what they are,' she said. 'You might be a collector, but you really need to get somebody with you who knows their stuff. Unfortunately, I'm not for hire.'

She turned and walked off, glancing at Macleod. He had a smug look on his face. However, Clarissa was worried. At the moment, they had found nothing that would implicate Harwich in the schemes that his bodyguard was involved in.

'So,' said Macleod, 'where are we at?'

'We've nearly had the whole house searched. And we're struggling.' Clarissa called Sabine over who gave a similar report. Clarissa toured the entire house, telling others to continue the search, even though they'd already covered those areas. Macleod was getting impatient, and Harwich was smiling.

202

'That little rat knows something,' said Macleod. 'He has sat here, getting more and more happy the longer this has gone on and you've found nothing.'

'I know,' said Clarissa.

'And you told me it wasn't here.'

'It's not here. Not where we have been,' said Clarissa. 'He has it, though. You can tell from the man. You can tell from his reactions.'

'Indeed,' said Macleod. 'I agree with you. I think he has it. But does he have it here?'

Clarissa sat down for a moment on a chair on one side of the room she was in. This was his prized room. This is where he kept the best. Clarissa looked around at the items. For a decent collector, yes, these were good items. There was some rarity to them. But there was nothing in here that said, 'I've got this; no one else has.'

A true collector wouldn't give two hoots about showing them off. A true collector has to have it, has to look at it themself, almost takes pleasure because no one else gets to look. There was something else here, she was sure of it. He was a man in a secret society, a man dealing with them, a man of considerable influence. He could get items that would be hard to get, items that were stolen.

One of the items in here was stolen. That was the failsafe; that was the one they could charge him on and then he'd come up and say the dealer did this and the dealer had sold it to him. She was convinced that's what would happen. It wasn't one he'd acquired; it was one he had bought accidentally, to clear his name if he was ever accused. No, this wasn't the real collection. She stood up by Macleod.

'This isn't his proper collection. This isn't the stuff that he truly wants to own.'

'But where does he show off the stuff that he truly wants to own then?' asked Macleod.

'That's the point, Seoras. He doesn't want to show it off. The stuff that a person like this wants to own are the things that you can't get hold of. If he could steal the Mona Lisa, he'd keep it and tell no one. He'd come down and look at it every day, self-satisfied because he owned it and nobody else had it.'

'What's the point of that?' asked Macleod.

'It's ownership,' said Clarissa. 'When you have so much money that money doesn't matter, you need to own other things. You need to possess. He's probably got a wife that's half his age. Thinks he owns her, too.'

'Actually,' said Macleod, 'his wife's the same age as him.'

'He's probably got other women he owns somewhere else. Or maybe that doesn't float his boat,' said Clarissa. 'Maybe what floats his boat is the artwork. He's not clever though. Really isn't. He can't spot a forgery.'

Clarissa stopped and looked over at a mirror on the wall. She strode over and examined the edge. She was joined suddenly by Harwich.

'Beautiful, isn't it,' he said. 'Very old. Very, very old. I bet you can't guess where it's from.'

'Give me a moment,' said Clarissa. She stood and leaned forward. Her eyes roamed around it. 'Solihull,' she said. Harwich laughed.

'Solihull in Birmingham? You are a preposterous woman. I thought you knew your stuff. It is from Spain. I have the history of it. It's all laid out, all about it.'

'It's not from Spain,' she said. She looked down at Harwich's hands, clearly beginning to sweat. 'The edges are wrong,' she said. 'Well, if you're going to get somebody to do a copy, you need to make sure that they understand how the things were formed in the first place. But, if you can't form it like that because it has to perform a second function,' said Clarissa, 'then so be it. Trouble is, you might get somebody come along who actually knows what they're talking about.

'In fairness, I think Sabine would have caught this. I'm disappointed she hasn't so far. But then again, she'd have to hear from you where it was from. This is from Solihall.'

The man looked at her. 'You are preposterous.'

For a moment, she stood and thought. And then she said to him, 'Would you mind taking your jacket off?'

'Why?'

'Just a brief experiment,' she said.

'It's not an unreasonable request,' Macleod chimed in. 'No harm is there in taking a jacket off?'

'Well, this is highly irregular,' said the man. But he took his jacket off, handing it over to a servant, who approached suddenly. He then turned back to Clarissa. 'And now you see me in my shirt. Is there anything else you'd like me to take off?'

'Roll your sleeves up, please,' said Clarissa.

The man looked at her. Macleod interjected. 'What is the harm in rolling your sleeves up? If you don't, we'll go down to the station and I'll get you to roll them up there.'

Harwich scowled but rolled his sleeves up. On the inside of his arms were tattoos.

'I don't like to show these. Got them in my younger day.'

Suddenly, Clarissa reached forward. She grabbed his right arm and held it up to the mirror suddenly. He tried to snatch it away, but Macleod reached forward too, both of them allowing the painted arm to remain in front of the mirror. There was a click. At the rear of the room, one of the panels of the wall suddenly pushed slightly ajar.

'If you look at the arm, sir,' Clarissa said to Macleod, 'you'll note that in the middle of that tattoo are certain shapes. They seem to me to be of a similar vein as to the tattoo found on his bodyguard. It's cleverly hidden, but the colour of it differs from the rest of the tattoo and the mirror picks up. It allows Harwich to go into this room at the back. Can we see your real collection?'

Macleod looked at Harwich, showing he should enter the room. The three of them walked in. Clarissa smiled.

'This is more like it. Detective Chief Inspector, let me introduce you to a few works here. Stolen, stolen, stolen, stolen. You've got maybe twenty in here. I've had ten seconds, and I can tell you that seven of them are stolen so far. If I go through the rest, I'm sure there'll be more than that. But look here in the middle.' There was a wooden table with a glass holder in the middle, on top of which sat a diamond. 'That is the Esoteric Tear.'

Macleod began to laugh. 'Got you, Harwich,' he said. 'Got you. Well done, Clarissa. Well done, Detective Inspector Urquhart. You have nailed him. Your first case, and you've bagged a big one. We'll lock you up for the theft if we can't do you for any of the rest of it,' said Macleod to him. 'We've got you banged to rights,'

Clarissa was now holding the Esoteric Tear in her hand. She looked at it closely. 'I'm afraid not, sir,' she said to Macleod. She turned and saw Macleod's mouth drop. But his shock was nothing as that of Lord Harwich's.

'It's a fake.'

Chapter 25

'I'm not sure this is a good idea,' said Patterson. 'Don't get me wrong, boss. I enjoy your company and all that, but we've been sitting in this green car at Findhorn for how long? Four or five days now?'

'Well, between us, we've been here a week.'

'Sabine seemed pretty keen to get back down to Glasgow. I think the idea of staying in the hotel has run its course for her.'

'Well, I get that. We used to be away for quite a time with the murder squad. Anyway, I'm not done yet,' said Clarissa.

'Why do you think Ali Ralston is definitely going to come here?'

'Because it's the only thing I've got. When she contacted Gillan, she came here. This is where they met. She had no idea that we were watching her. Nobody knew we followed her. It's a safe meeting place. She still has the diamond, and she's going to try to sell it on. Ali Ralston will not want it for anything. She'll just want rid of it.'

'She might have run already.'

'She'll need the money to run,' said Clarissa. 'The money they'll give her will be a phenomenal amount. Remember, she's got no job, and she's got no life. Having had a taste of what these groups are like, she'll want rid of that diamond, and get far away.'

'She's done well, though,' said Patterson. 'There hasn't been sight nor sound of her.'

'No, there hasn't, so she's gone to ground pretty well. If I was her, I'd have done that too. I'd have stayed out of sight for at least three or four days, then maybe try to contact the other side. Tell them she still had it. Arrange a pickup then. Findhorn is a place she knows. It's out of the way, and yet it's near enough to Inverness that she can get here quickly. It doesn't have to be a lot of discussion; it just has to be a brief exchange and a diamond.

'Last time, they obviously didn't trust Gillan with the money. This time she's going to ask for it up front. She's going to tell them just to give it to her and she'll hand it over. Gillan last time was organising everything. Maybe she had to be talked into it. Maybe that's what they did in the first place, sought her out. After all, she was romantic with Gillan. Maybe that was an act on his part. Maybe he wooed her to get her to do it.'

'I'm not sure we could confirm that,' said Patterson.

'No, Pats, of course we can't. It's all supposition. But it works. You've got to remember, if she's been taken in by Gillan, she's just seen him die. Romantic interest. She's going to want to run. She really is going to want to run. But she can't run without the money. It's hard. Especially against organisations like this. She's got to be scared witless by them.'

'She could have come to us.'

'Gillan would have told her about the influence they had because both sides will have the influence.'

'What about Harwich?' asked Patterson.

'Sabines watching him. Watching some of his people. He's

in trouble anyway at the moment. We've got enough artwork that he will get lifted. Things he'd stolen over the years. We'll not pin the murders on him. Too difficult. It probably wasn't him, anyway. I don't know if we'll ever get that sorted.'

'The thing is that if we get Ali Ralston here, the diamond goes into police custody. It will then go somewhere and they'll still go after it. This circus will continue, won't it?' said Patterson.

'That's right. And if she runs with it, the circus will continue elsewhere. And there'll be a trio of bodies behind it. The very thing that Macleod didn't want.'

'There's not a lot you can do to prevent that though, is there?'

'You'd think not. Heads up, Pats,' said Clarissa suddenly. 'Look over there. She's a fine-looking girl, isn't she?'

Clarissa was staring at Ali Ralston stepping out of a car that she hadn't been seen in before. It was probably a hire car, and the woman was dressed almost entirely in black. She had a bobble hat on, hiding her hair, and some sunglasses. Clarissa nearly laughed. Why would you be wearing sunglasses today? There was no sun.

'Shall I go get her?' asked Patterson. 'Do we cut her off?'

'I'll go,' said Clarissa. 'She's likely to be here early. I'll have a word. Just stay here in the car in case she makes a run for it. But I don't think she will.'

Clarissa stepped out of her little green car, threw her shawl over her shoulder again, and walked quietly and calmly along the street towards Ali Ralston. The woman's face dropped when she saw her. She went to turn but Clarissa gave a quick shout of, 'Don't; we're everywhere; you need to stop.'

Clarissa continued to walk forward, and Ralston was shaking. As Clarissa arrived in front of her, she reached up and took the sunglasses off Ralston's face. She folded them and handed them to her.

'If you're going to disguise yourself, don't put shades on when there's no need for them. You're an idiot or you're the one they're looking for.'

'They'll kill me,' said Ralston. 'They'll kill me here if they see me with you.'

'Give me the diamond. Give me the Esoteric Tear,' said Clarissa.

'I don't have it,' said Ali Ralston. 'You saw Gillan in the barn. You saw me.'

'I saw Gillan give it to someone. That someone gave it to Lord Harwich. He was mighty annoyed when I turned up with my boss and searched his place and found it. Only, it was a fake. What set Gillan off? Why was he bothered? What was he—'

'He wasn't convinced that they would just let me walk away with the money. He thought his side would kill me.'

'And yet you're here, about to trade that diamond for money again with them.'

'I have to get away but I have no money. I give it to them, and the other side will go after them, not me.'

'No, they won't. They'll go after you because they won't realise that the other side has got it. And the other side will in no way tell them they've got it. The only time they'll realise that you haven't got it is after they've killed you and searched everything that you own. Give the diamond to me,' said Clarissa.

'But they won't believe you unless I go into custody, unless I'm—'

'Arrested for it? And even then they might, because you've spoken with Gillan and seen things. Go far away, Ali. Go far away. You hear me? I'll make this go away. I'll get them off your back, but you never come back. When I say go away, I mean Australia; I mean New Zealand. I mean Ali Ralston dies today. If you want to live, Ali Ralston dies.'

The woman looked at Clarissa. 'He said he could make it work. He said we'd go off and live together.'

'He might have meant it as well. Maybe he fell for you once he'd made contact. That's why they sent him out originally, because you were organising this tour and they wanted to get the diamond. You let them in, didn't you? You took it. Nobody broke into that trailer. You did it on the quiet. You handed it to Gillan, and he drove off. It would have worked really, really smoothly if I hadn't interrupted him. And then strangely, he gives all the diamonds back, and that's where it really got interesting for me.'

'How do I know you won't come after me?'

'I want this ended. You giving me the diamond means I can end it.'

Ali Ralston reached inside of her jacket pocket and then handed something over to Clarissa. She took it in her palm, and stared at the diamond. She held it up briefly to the sky for a moment and then she put it in her pocket.

'Go,' said Clarissa. 'Nobody here will stop you. The person you're meant to meet isn't here yet. I'll make sure they know there's a police presence. That'll scare them off. They'll lie low for a while, expecting you to do the same. They'll know I haven't got you, but you haven't surfaced either. Therefore, you're in hiding and they'll wait. I think you'll have about a week to get away. If you want, I can put you in contact with some people who can help.'

Clarissa took a small piece of paper out of her pocket. 'Don't read this here. Just give me your hand and I'll shake it and you take the paper.'

'Do these people work for the police?'

'No,' said Clarissa. 'However, they have had some financial recompense to assist you in getting out of the country and starting up again. I'm sorry this happened to you, Ali. Go make a life for yourself.'

Clarissa reached forward with her hand. Ali reached forward with hers and they shook, the paper transferring. Ali turned back to her car and drove off. Clarissa, meanwhile, simply stood where she was. She waved over at Patterson once Ali Ralston had driven past him, and he drove the little green car a short distance up to the car park.

'Get over, it's my car,' said Clarissa. She sat down in the driver's seat as he shifted.

'Where's Ali Ralston going?'

'Away, for good.'

'But she's got the diamond,' said Patterson.

'She had it.' Clarissa reached inside her pocket, pulled it out, and showed it to Patterson. 'You see, Pats, I've got it now.'

'Macleod will want to know how you got it.'

'No, he'll want to know how I lost it.'

'What do you mean?'

'We're going to sit here for a bit. The person she was going to trade with is going to turn up and then he's going to disappear again. That's because he'll realise that the police are sitting here rather ineffectively in a small, green sports car. He'll probably guess who we are. You're going to look very official sitting beside me too, just so he gets the picture. After that, there'll be a report going out that I saw Ali Ralston. However, we failed to intercept her. Instead there was a scuffle and the

Esoteric Tear is out there.' She pointed out to sea.

'Where are you going to put it for real?' asked Patterson.

'You don't seriously think I'm going to tell you that?'

They sat in silence, waiting another half an hour before a van drove past. It drove four times round Findhorn before disappearing. Clarissa smiled.

'Well, they got the message,' she said and started up the car. She drove along, then stopped by the sea. She walked along the coast, looking out to the Moray Firth, Patterson following her.

'Where are you going?' he asked.

'Macleod won't understand this,' she said. 'But he said to me that this wouldn't stop. He saw my point. We needed to put a stop to it. I'm putting a stop to it,' she said.

Clarissa took the diamond out of her pocket and showed it one last time to Patterson. She looked left and right along the coast, stared out in front of her, and could see no one watching. She bent round, twisted as hard as she could, before flinging her arm round and throwing the gemstone as hard as she could out into the Moray Firth.

'Won't it come to shore at some point?' asked Patterson.

'Of course it will. Nobody's going to identify it, though. That's if they find it. It might go under the sand. Unfortunately, it's gone out there. Where we had the scuffle was some distance along. It's lost, and it'll stop the killing. It'll stop the hunt for a while. If they get a boat or search through the sand, so be it. Stuff them. Maybe it'll stay lost for ten years, and they'll realise the end time hasn't come. And they'll forget it all and go off on some other crazy scheme.'

Patterson stood looking out to the sea, and he nodded. 'I probably wouldn't have done that.'

'That's why you're here, Pats. You're here to learn.'

* * *

Macleod watched Clarissa leaving his office, picked up his cup of coffee, and drank from it. He turned and stared out of his window. Ali Ralston had turned up. Ali Ralston had run away. Clarissa had caught up, and they'd had a fight. The diamond had slipped out and tumbled off into the sea. Ali Ralston had legged it. She was remarkably quick and agile, had floored Patterson and was away. Everything was resolved.

They'd look for Ali Ralston in the coming weeks, try to find her. They'd maybe even send people down to look for the diamond. Macleod smiled to himself as he drank his coffee.

'What a total pack of lies,' he said to himself. But she closed it off, and we got Harwich. He smiled. We got the bodyguard, but the main thing she did was close it off.

Macleod sipped from his cup again. He'd had enough of secret organisations. After all, he'd suffered at their hands before. He looked forward to the panic on their faces, knowing the apocalypse was coming and there was no way out now. Of course it had been a gamble, he thought, giving her this. She wasn't daft, but she could work close to the bone, his Rottweiler. He was beginning to like the idea of the arts side. It was fun. Maybe as much as being in the murder squad.

Read on to discover the Patrick Smythe series!

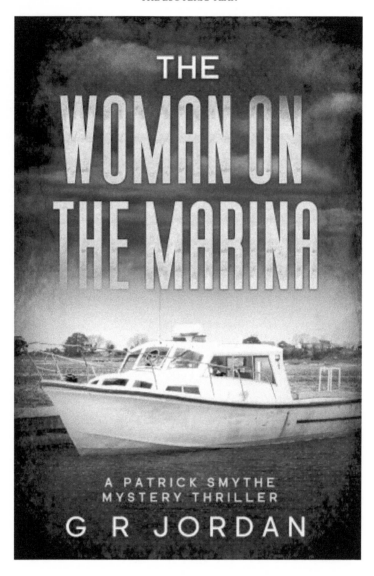

Patrick Smythe is a former Northern Irish policeman who after suffering an amputation after a bomb blast, takes to the sea between the west coast of Scotland and his homeland to ply his trade as a private investigator. Join Paddy as he tries to work to his own ethics while knowing how to bend the rules he once enforced. Working from his beloved motorboat 'Craigantlet', Paddy decides to rescue a drug mule in this short story from the pen of G R Jordan.

Join G R Jordan's monthly newsletter about forthcoming releases and special writings for his tribe of avid readers and then receive your free Patrick Smythe short story.

Go to https://bit.ly/PatrickSmythe for your Patrick Smythe journey to start!

About the Author

GR Jordan is a self-published author who finally decided at forty that in order to have an enjoyable lifestyle, his creative beast within would have to be unleashed. His books mirror that conflict in life where acts of decency contend with self-promotion, goodness stares in horror at evil, and kindness blindsides us when we at our worst. Corrupting our world with his parade of wondrous and horrific characters, he highlights everyday tensions with fresh eyes whilst taking his methodical, intelligent mainstays on a roller-coaster ride of dilemmas, all the while suffering the banter of their provocative sidekicks.

A graduate of Loughborough University where he masqueraded as a chemical engineer but ultimately played American football, Gary had worked at changing the shape of cereal flakes and pulled a pallet truck for a living. Watching vegetables freeze at -40'C was another career highlight and he was also one of the Scottish Highlands "blind" air traffic controllers.

These days he has graduated to answering a telephone to people in trouble before telephoning other people to sort it out.

Having flirted with most places in the UK, he is now based in the Isle of Lewis in Scotland where his free time is spent between raising a young family with his wife, writing, figuring out how to work a loom and caring for a small flock of chickens. Luckily, his writing is influenced by his varied work and life experience as the chickens have not been the poetical inspiration he had hoped for!

You can connect with me on:

🌐 https://grjordan.com

f https://facebook.com/carpetlessleprechaun

Subscribe to my newsletter:

✉ https://bit.ly/PatrickSmythe

Also by G R Jordan

G R Jordan writes across multiple genres including crime, dark and action adventure fantasy, feel good fantasy, mystery thriller and horror fantasy. Below is a selection of his work. Whilst all books are available across online stores, signed copies are available at his personal shop.

A Rock 'n' Roll Murder (Highlands & Islands Detective Book 33)
https://grjordan.com/product/a-rock-n-roll-murder
A rock 'n' roll stalwart is burnt with his guitar. A royalty's war erupts as his music returns to the top. Can DI McGrath find the musician hitting a bum note?

Donal Diamond, the eighties legend, is found in his burnt-out studio with his guitar in hand. As news spreads of the rocker's demise, his music stock's value rises and the fight for his estate begins. In a field her DCI cannot fathom, Hope McGrath must navigate nostalgia and genuine hate to find out who sacrificed the sacred cow for greater riches in the morning.

It's never one—it's all for the money!

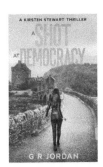

Kirsten Stewart Thrillers
https://grjordan.com/product/a-shot-at-democracy

Join Kirsten Stewart on a shadowy ride through the underbelly of the Highlands of Scotland where among the beauty and splendour of the majestic landscape lies corruption and intrigue to match any city. From murders to extortion, missing children to criminals operating above the law, the Highland former detective must learn a tougher edge to her work as she puts her own life on the line to protect those who cannot defend themselves.

Having left her beloved murder investigation team far behind, Kirsten has to battle personal tragedy and loss while adapting to a whole new way of executing her duties where your mistakes are your own. As Kirsten comes to terms with working with the new team, she often operates as the groups solo field agent, placing herself in danger and trouble to rescue those caught on the dark side of life. With action packed scenes and tense scenarios of murder and greed, the Kirsten Stewart thrillers will have you turning page after page to see your favourite Scottish lass home!

There's life after Macleod, but a whole new world of death!

Jac's Revenge (A Jack Moonshine Thriller #1)
https://grjordan.com/product/jacs-revenge
An unexpected hit makes Debbie a widow. The attention of her man's killer spawns a brutal yet classy alter ego. But how far can you play the game before it takes over your life?

All her life, Debbie Parlor lived in her man's shadow, knowing his work was never truly honest. She turned her head from news stories and rumours. But when he was disposed of for his smile to placate a rival crime lord, Jac Moonshine was born. And when Debbie is paid compensation for her loss like her car was written off, Jac decides that enough is enough.

Get on board with this tongue-in-cheek revenge thriller that will make you question how far you would go to avenge a loved one, and how much you would enjoy it!

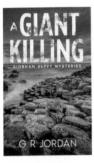

A Giant Killing (Siobhan Duffy Mysteries #1)

https://grjordan.com/product/a-giant-killing

A body lies on the Giant's boot. Discord, as the master of secrets has been found. Can former spy Siobhan Duffy find the killer before they execute her former colleagues?

When retired operative Siobhan Duffy sees the killing of her former master in the paper, her unease sends her down a path of discovery and fear. Aided by her young housekeeper and scruff of a gardener, Siobhan begins a quest to discover the reason for her spy boss' death and unravels a can of worms today's masters would rather keep closed. But in a world of secrets, the difference between revenge and simple, if brutal, housekeeping becomes the hardest truth to know.

The past is a child who never leaves home!